Escape from Zion

In these short stories by ex-Mormon author Johnny Townsend, parents hire men to pose as the Three Nephites to teach their children the Book of Mormon is true. A shy single woman meets the man of her dreams at an endoscopy party.

An anti-Mormon mob threatens a church outing. A deceased sinner plots to break out of Spirit Prison. Aliens visiting the UN reveal that God really does live on the planet Kolob. Mormons survive the zombie apocalypse because of their two-year supply of food. A young couple desperately try to escape after America becomes a theocracy.

Another fun collection from the author of *Recommended Daily Humanity* and *Please Evacuate*.

Praise for Johnny Townsend

In *Zombies for Jesus,* "Townsend isn't writing satire, but deeply emotional and revealing portraits of people who are, with a few exceptions, quite lovable."

Kel Munger, *Sacramento News and Review*

In *Sex among the Saints,* "Townsend writes with a deadpan wit and a supple, realistic prose that's full of psychological empathy….he takes his protagonists' moral struggles seriously and invests them with real emotional resonance."

Kirkus Reviews

Inferno in the French Quarter: The UpStairs Lounge Fire is "a gripping account of all the horrors that transpired that night, as well as a respectful remembrance of the victims."

Terry Firma, Patheos

"Johnny Townsend's 'Partying with St. Roch' [in the anthology *Latter-Gay Saints*] tells a beautiful, haunting tale."

Kent Brintnall, Out in Print: Queer Book Reviews

Selling the City of Enoch is "sharply intelligent…pleasingly complex…The stories are full of…doubters, but there's no vindictiveness in these pages; the characters continuously poke holes in Mormonism's more extravagant absurdities, but they take very little pleasure in doing so….Many of Townsend's stories…have a provocative edge to them, but this [book] displays a great deal of insight as well…a playful, biting and surprisingly warm collection."

Kirkus Reviews

Gayrabian Nights is "an allegorical tour de force…a hard-core emotional punch."

Gay. Guy. Reading and Friends

The Washing of Brains has "A lovely writing style, and each story [is] full of unique, engaging characters….immensely entertaining."

Rainbow Awards

In *Dead Mankind Walking*, "Townsend writes in an energetic prose that balances crankiness and humor….A rambunctious volume of short, well-crafted essays…"

Kirkus Reviews

Escape from Zion

Johnny Townsend

Print ISBN: 979-8-9883389-2-5
Ebook ISBN: 979-8-9883389-3-2

[Selected stories from *Lying for the Lord, Despots of Deseret, Dragons of the Book of Mormon,* and *Mormon Fairy Tales.*]

Printed on acid-free paper.

2023

First Edition

Cover design by Denis Lenzzi

Contents

Spirit Prison Blues

"Who died and made you boss?" said Ian testily.

"I did," Marcus replied. He looked at the picture on the wall of the Salt Lake temple. On the opposite wall was one of the San Diego temple.

"Well, I'm dead, too. When do I get to start making rules around here?"

"As soon as we pass the parole board tribunal, I guess."

Ian sighed and stared gloomily at Marcus. "So what's on the agenda today?"

Marcus looked over at Ian and wished again he had a different cellmate. They weren't technically in cells, of course. The doors were only locked in the evenings. But they weren't allowed to go anywhere without their assigned companion. Since they never needed to go to the bathroom, this meant they never even got a few minutes alone throughout the entire day. Marcus was with Ian and his negativity every second of what was apparently an intermediate eternity.

"We've got the library this morning," Marcus began.

"Ugh."

"And then film class."

"Oh my god."

"Then the museum."

"Of course."

"But tonight instead of classes, there's a special concert."

Ian looked at him sharply. "Who is it this time? Not George Osmond again?"

Marcus shrugged. "It's better than the Mormon Tabernacle Choir emeritus."

"Not by much."

"Would you rather the Ogden First Ward choir again?"

Ian stared at the floor. "No," he said. "I guess not."

Marcus and Ian got dressed. It seemed strange that in Spirit Prison, where they'd gone after their deaths because they weren't Mormon, they'd be allowed, or actually constrained, to sleep in the nude. Marcus was pretty sure it was only to emphasize the fact they no longer had bodies. Marcus could see his dick, could touch it, but he couldn't actually feel it or get an erection.

It was depressing, but every evening just before lights out, they were told to take a good look in the mirror, and if they wanted their bodies back anytime soon, they'd better repent and hope someone did some proxy work in the temple for them so they could be resurrected sooner rather than later.

Marcus and Ian trudged down the hallway, buzzed out of the building, and walked across the campus to the library.

Marcus remembered the shock he'd felt at being told he wasn't in heaven. He'd been an activist for ACORN most of his adult life, had helped to register poor Black and Latino voters, had worked to improve conditions for immigrant workers, had sought to increase the minimum wage, and had been a union organizer. He'd believed in God, attended a liberation theology church, and had spent his life helping the poor and working class.

So why hadn't he gone to heaven?

"Actually, *no one* goes to heaven when they die," the warden told him that first day. "It's just that the good Mormons go to Paradise."

"And Paradise isn't heaven?" Marcus had asked in confusion.

The warden shook his head. "It's a resort where Mormons go until Judgment Day." He shrugged. "But I suppose it's kind of like the five semi-finalists of the Miss America pageant. You already have to score pretty high to get it. It's only the exact order of the final reward that's still a mystery."

Marcus and Ian scanned their badges at the library entrance. Everywhere you went, you were monitored to determine how good you were being. All the data were collected to be analyzed at the end of each week, and you met with an officer to discuss your progress. Marcus had to set short- and long-term goals so he'd be ready for the parole board when the time came. It irked Marcus to no end. He felt like he was in kindergarten, being told when he could and couldn't take a nap.

At least they still had sleep up here. It was the only respite he ever got. Apparently, even spirit bodies had spirit neurons that needed time to recuperate. They were allowed exactly eight hours a night to sleep. Then at the crack of dawn, they had to jump out of bed.

But there was no coffee, no matter how much he longed for it.

Marcus hadn't been able to determine exactly where they were, but it seemed to still be Earth, just another dimension. He could still see the moon at night, could still see Venus up in the sky. He'd overheard two guards say once that an inmate had snuck back to the other side for almost an entire day before being discovered and had been severely punished as a result.

"Good morning, Marcus," said the librarian, a vapid woman named Marcy, smiling cheerily. "And Ian. What'll it be today?" She waved her arms toward the stacks. "We have Glenn Beck's latest book. And Spencer Kimball has just written a new one."

Marcus grimaced. He'd learned the names of all the Mormon leaders of the past century and a half and had read two dozen books by them since arriving in this place three months ago. In essence, Marcy had explained that the only books available were whatever might be found in Deseret bookstores on Earth, tomes written by Mormons, new books by Isaiah or Elijah, or occasional "edgy" material like Jane Austen, *Lassie*, *Pollyanna*, or *Anne of Green Gables*.

Marcus typed *Northanger Abbey* into the computer, which didn't look all that different from an Apple, but he heard Marcy sniff pointedly, and he instead ended up with a slim volume called *Fatherhood* by Rex Pinegar, whoever he was. There were still more names to learn.

Marcus had never been a father as far as he knew. He hadn't wanted to bring children into such a corrupt world, hadn't wanted to take time away from trying to improve the world. But he'd heard since his arrival how important it was to seem like a family man, so he thought he'd give the book a try.

As he started off toward the couches, Marcy called after him in her stage whisper, "Have the best of all possible days…and smile!"

Marcus closed his eyes for a moment but then did force a smile through gritted teeth. He didn't like being ordered to be in a good mood, but he remembered yet again that everything here was monitored.

Posted in his and Ian's cell was a sign that proclaimed, "Attitude Counts!" He'd tried to remove it his first day there, but it seemed adhered to the wall with some kind of superglue. A guard had passed by the cell later, pointed at the sign, and wagged his finger.

Marcus read for the next three hours. There was nothing else to do. He'd have to keep reading for two more as well. Once on the couches, there was a strict rule against talking. You could only read and reflect on what you were learning. The history was moderately interesting, but the theology was ludicrous. If Marcus hadn't wanted three children brought into a miserable world on Earth, he sure as hell didn't want to father six or seven billion spirit children who would all be forced onto another planet of similar misery.

Of course, chances were slim he'd ever have that opportunity. Only those who made it to the top degree of the Celestial Kingdom became gods. If a person never had the chance to accept the gospel in life, they could hear about it in Spirit Prison, accept, and then, based on how they'd acted in life in relation to which true principles they'd been exposed to, they could still qualify here.

But Marcus had turned Mormon missionaries away from his door twice. He'd campaigned for Al Gore and later Barack Obama, voting against Mitt Romney. He'd given money to support abortion rights and universal healthcare. He might be eligible for one of the lesser kingdoms eventually, but only if he repented.

And he was still in no mood to repent.

Repentance implied you thought you'd done wrong, and Marcus wasn't sure he had, despite all that he'd learned here.

Marcus looked over at Ian. His cellmate was reading a book about *The Importance of Obedience*. He looked absorbed.

Marcus rolled his eyes. He couldn't wait till Saturday, when they had visiting hours. Then he was able to visit his friends and relatives who had died before him. The problem, of course, was that these visits were monitored, too. If you spent too much time with a rebellious prisoner, it was written down.

Marcus closed his eyes, thinking of Nancy. She'd been his girlfriend years ago, in college. While Marcus sometimes smoked pot, he'd never tried hard drugs, like Nancy did. One evening, he came home from work to find her overdosed on the bed. He'd always regretted not being able to tell her goodbye, so he'd looked her up once he arrived in prison.

Nancy wasn't in a regular cellblock, though. She was in a detox center. The thing was, naturally, that she was permanently in a state of withdrawal. Without a body, she couldn't really detox, and Marcus had been horrified to see her shaking and screaming, and to realize she'd been doing this for twenty years now. When Marcus protested to the guard, demanding help, the woman had simply said, "Too bad. So sad. That's what she gets for sinning."

Marcus had tried to hit her, but without a body himself, he'd been unable. Still, the guard wrote down the incident in her tablet, and his case manager had berated him at length during his next weekly appraisal.

He continued to see Nancy first thing every Saturday morning, though he could only force himself to stay for an hour. The other inmates had told him Nancy probably wouldn't be resurrected till *after* the Millennium, so she'd be like this at least another thousand years. "It's not that anyone *wants* her to suffer," one grinning doofus said. "It's just that there are natural consequences to certain actions. It's not as if God is *cruel*."

But Marcus began to wonder. The religion classes ran from 6:00 till 9:30 every evening, unless there was a concert, and the more he learned, the less impressed he became. A volunteer teacher from Paradise came to see him every night, trying to earn a few extra points post-life because he was apparently a borderline case between the highest degree of the Terrestrial and the lowest of the Celestial.

But this guy, Terrence, insisted that gays were damned no matter how real they thought their love was. He said there was a hierarchy in heaven, that while technically a woman could become a goddess, she was still subject to her god-husband. You could have only one ultimate ruler in any universe. You never heard an Old Testament prophet saying, "God's wife told him to tell me to tell you…" And no one could become a god at all, man or woman, without being married.

But Marcus had never married. He'd always thought it too stifling for both the husband and the wife. He was horrified to think he'd now have to accept an eternal marriage that would *never* end.

"The problem," Terrence had explained, shaking his head sadly, "is that you were never married in life. So it's not as if someone can just go to the temple to do proxy work for the dead for you. You'll have to meet someone here. And *if* you qualify in other respects, you can be resurrected in time to get married in the Millennium." He shook his head again. "But it won't look good on your record."

Marcus heard a tapping noise and turned to look at the librarian. Marcy had seen he was daydreaming and wanted him to get back to his studies. He nodded and looked at the pages once more, but not before watching her write something down in a notebook.

Marcus gritted his teeth again. Then he quietly slipped his own pen out of his pocket. The inmates had been given pens and notebooks so they could take notes about the books they read or films they saw. Marcus hadn't written much so far, but now he uncapped his pen. He glanced over at Marcy, who was talking to another inmate, and he opened the book to the middle. "Fuck fatherhood," he wrote in long, bold lines.

Finally, reading period was over, and there was a half-hour break before the afternoon film session began. "What'd you think?" Marcus asked, standing outside under a tree and really, really wishing he had a cigarette.

"I'm seriously missing my Stephen King," Ian said in a subdued voice.

Why? Weren't they living a horror story themselves?

"And I wish I could have my Faye Kellerman back." Marcus paused. What he wouldn't give to read about a carefully plotted murder, something he might try to reenact. *Some* of the staff here, after all, had bodies. "Do you suppose we could start a petition?"

He was half joking, but Ian gasped.

Marcus was irritated. "Who cares if we have a few points deducted?"

Ian shook his head. "This isn't like cramming for some college exam that determines your grade for the course. This is for *forever*. I'm not about to louse it up."

Marcus looked at Ian closely, evaluating how much he could say. "I think," he began, "I may try to sneak out of the cellblock tonight."

"What?"

"Try to get back to the other side."

"Whatever for?"

Marcus shrugged. "I don't know. I still won't be able to drink a beer or kiss a woman, but…"

"But what?"

Marcus shrugged again. "I don't know," he repeated. "I don't even know that I'd try to materialize and warn people. What would I tell them? I don't want to become Mormon even now. There's no reason I should tell anyone back there to get baptized."

Ian tilted his head. "Don't you *want* to be on God's side? Haven't you *seen* how awful Lucifer is?"

Marcus nodded. One of the first films they'd viewed was a documentary about Satan, how the evil spirits who'd followed him never obtained a body, so when apostates were sent to join them, everyone jumped into the bodies and fought over them. They were in continual spasms from the competing spirits, and there were physical fist fights between the bodies, as groups of spirits in one tried to subdue or rape the group of spirits in the other. It looked like hell.

Marcus smiled for a moment at the unintended pun but then frowned. What *did* he want out of eternity? To sit in a meadow and listen to Pearl Jam forever? You had to do *something*, but was godhood the answer? Even among Mormons, it was only a tiny elite who achieved that. Most people, even Mormons, had to be content with eternal limitation, not eternal progression. It somehow didn't seem fair. Judging the few years of life out of an eternity of existence was like asking a five-year-old who could barely concentrate to take a test that would determine the course of the next seventy years of his life.

"Well, *I* think we'd better get with the program," Ian said. "There are degrees of unhappiness. And being Mormon throughout eternity has got to be better than the alternative."

Marcus wasn't so sure, but he didn't say anything else. He listened as Ian told him what he'd learned that morning, and soon it was time to head to the theater. Here, there were a few minutes to chat with other inmates, but too soon, the lights dimmed and the film started.

Today's first show was a summary of the Spanish conquest of the Incas. They weren't watching a re-creation, of course, but the actual events, the actual people. There was a voice-over, like Cecil B. DeMille in *The Greatest Show on Earth*, talking about how the Lamanites had fallen away and were ripe for destruction.

The voice-over seemed to be in English, but the voices of the Incas were in a Native American dialect, and the Spanish soldiers spoke Spanish. Yet even though there were no subtitles, somehow Marcus understood every word of the movie.

After the film, there was a break during which everyone had to take a quiz. The questions were multiple choice, but they never asked much about the actual events themselves. One of the questions today, for example, was:

To what did the Incas owe their destruction?

> A. Personal depravity
> B. An evil religion
> C. Social injustice
> D. A and B only
> E. B and C only
> F. All of the above

Marcus circled C, but when the tests were graded at the end of the session, he learned he'd been mistaken. The teacher drew a smiley face with a frown on his paper.

Next came a film about the early Christians as they fell away from the gospel and into apostasy. It seemed to be a major theme today. After a quiz on the Thessalonians, Marcus whispered to Ian, "I'm going for it tonight."

"No!"

"What's the worst they can do? Lock me up?"

There was one last, shorter film about how the Reorganized Church of Jesus Christ of Latter-day Saints broke away from the main group after Joseph Smith's assassination, and then finally film class was over. Marcus felt like a boy again in math class. "When am I ever going to need algebra?" he'd complained to the teacher.

Now he knew the answer to that question. If he was going to create worlds, he had to know every fact of biology, physics, chemistry, calculus, and every other science. And he supposed he needed all these lessons about human nature, about right and wrong, too.

But one thing confused him. In life, Marcus had often felt there wasn't just black and white; there were lots of shades of gray. How could God be *more* complex than humans and yet have a *simpler* world view? Why wasn't there *more* complexity in making decisions now?

There was a fifteen-minute break during which Marcus tried to talk with a pretty female inmate. Marcus's spirit body was the image of his physical body at the age of twenty-four, when he'd been in his prime. But the woman still looked at him askance and turned away. There wasn't much chance he'd ever find a wife at this rate, with so little time for socializing.

The concert would give him more opportunities, though. He could mingle all evening. Maybe he could even find someone else who wanted to break out of prison, too.

At 6:30, everyone from his cellblock filed into a large auditorium. There was a little fidgeting and talking, but the guards quieted people down quickly. Marcus made a point of sitting near the end of a row so he could get up. He'd stand most of the evening, trying to talk to anyone who looked bored and thus open to dissent.

"Welcome, everyone," said a woman, beaming from the stage. "We trust you've had another productive day. But tonight, we want to reward you with a little concert from George Osmond." Marcus wondered if Ian was rolling his eyes, but he couldn't find Ian in the crowd. At least the event offered Marcus some relief from his companion's constant presence. No one was pleasant company twenty-four hours a day, every day. Marcus wondered again if he should even bother attempting marriage.

"George puts on a good show," the woman continued. "You'll be glad you died." She chuckled. "And next week…we have a special performance by the King family."

Marcus looked at his neighbor, mystified.

"Some of you older folks may remember Tina Cole from *My Three Sons*. Most of her family will be here. It'll be a real treat! So, everyone, be happy! And remember, you're a child of God!"

The lights dimmed, a spotlight shone on stage, and George Osmond walked out with a big smile. His first song was a cover of one of the covers his sons had sung, "He Ain't Heavy, He's My Brother." Marcus slipped out of his seat and started looking for anyone who might be unhappy to be there.

And there *was* someone. Another guy, an Asian, who kept looking at his naked wrist as if hoping to check the time. He was on the end of a row, too, and Marcus motioned to him. The guy nodded and stood up. He couldn't know what this was about, but that clearly didn't matter. Any excuse was a good one.

"You want to get out of here?" Marcus whispered.

"You mean skip the concert?"

"No, I mean, get *out* of here."

The man's eyes widened. Then he nodded. "I don't care what your plan is. I'm in."

Just then, four guards marched up to Marcus and his new friend. They had spirit handcuffs and slapped them on the two men.

"What's going on?" Marcus demanded. "Can't two guys hang out together at a concert?"

"Ian told us everything," said one of the guards. "He turned 'soul's evidence.' Admitted his own grumblings but gets points for turning you in."

"You're in big trouble now, mister," said one of the other guards.

"What about this guy?" asked Marcus. "*He* hasn't done anything."

"He's talking to *you*, isn't he?"

Marcus squinted. The guard looked like a young Joseph McCarthy. Marcus was led off in one direction by two of the guards, and the other man was led away by the others. Marcus ended up in a small room, sitting behind a table in a chair under a bright light that did not hurt his eyes. He looked off to the side.

"Oh my god," he said. "You have a one-way mirror!"

"Don't take the name of the Lord in vain."

"Fuck you."

One of the guards slapped the table in front of Marcus. "That's enough! We can throw you into Outer Darkness any time we want. Do you want to go to hell?"

Marcus looked at the two guards, and then glanced over at whoever might be watching through the mirror. "If there are degrees of heaven, there are degrees of hell, too. And this is certainly one of them."

The head guard gasped.

"You have a very rebellious spirit," the other guard said coolly, but Marcus thought he detected an almost admiring tone.

Marcus shrugged. "I don't like to see injustice."

"Injustice!" the first guard exclaimed. "We're giving you chance after chance after chance to repent!"

"You're giving me chance after chance after chance to become a Stepford saint. I want to choose my own path, not be forced to 'choose' the path you want me to take. What kind of freedom is that?"

"It's the only freedom there is," snapped the head guard. "You can take it or leave it."

Marcus thought for a moment.

"Well? What's it going to be?"

"I think your God is a bully," Marcus said calmly, eliciting horrified expressions from both guards. "And I think your Lucifer is a punk. I don't want to follow *either* of them."

"Those are your choices, buddy."

Marcus shook his head. "Why does this have to be a two-party system? I want an alternative. Maybe four or five alternatives."

There were more gasps.

"There's an eternity ahead of us," said Marcus. "And unlimited space. And that's only in this one dimension. There's certainly room for another team or two."

The head guard slapped the table again, but the other guard, while still angry, at the same time began to look confused.

Marcus glanced down at his cuffed hands, and suddenly, he experienced what he could only describe as a revelation. Pure knowledge entered his soul. He stood up and held his hands out in front of him.

"What are you doing?" the main guard asked nervously.

Marcus stared at his handcuffs a long moment, and then they unlocked and fell to the floor.

"Oh my god," whispered the second guard, taking the name of the Lord in vain himself.

"What did you do?" the head guard asked, angry but a little frightened now.

"You only have power over me if I concede that power to you," Marcus said. "I just realized that all this time, I've been complaining, but I've *let* you control me." He paused. "And that's not going to happen anymore."

"What—what are you going to do?" asked the guard.

Marcus thought for a moment. He had a lifetime of political activism and union organizing behind him. Perhaps he'd organize the inmates into a prison uprising. He rubbed his chin.

And maybe afterward, he'd go from universe to universe, creating spirit unions and pushing third party candidates. It was enough to keep him busy for a while. He could worry about what came after that later.

Marcus didn't answer the men but simply walked out of the room. The second guard ran after him, keeping his distance but looking almost hopeful. Marcus smiled and headed back for the cellblock. He walked up to the first cell and knocked on the door politely.

"Yes?" said a meek voice from inside.

"May I have permission to enter?" Marcus asked.

The door swung slowly, and a man whose mouth hung open stood staring at him.

"Do you want to go to heaven or hell?" asked Marcus bluntly.

"H-heaven," the man stammered. Now Marcus could see the guy's cellmate in the background, peering forward timidly. They'd clearly been in prison a long while.

"Yes," said Marcus, "but that's a close-ended question. How about we ask an open-ended one now?"

The man looked confused.

"*What* do you want out of eternity?"

The man looked at Marcus, at the guard, and even back at his cellmate before looking at Marcus again. "Is this a trick?"

"Nope." He smiled at the guard, who nodded his support. "We're making our *own* heaven." He offered his hand, and the man took it cautiously. "Mind if we come in and talk for a bit?"

The two cellmates looked at each other for a moment, communicating silently, and then opened the door wide, motioning him to enter. Marcus smiled and walked inside.

Getting Zeppoli from Derek

"Xtronical," I said, answering the phone on the first ring. "This is Ronette. How may I help you?" I'd been the receptionist here at the computer game company for just two weeks and was eager to be the best receptionist I could be.

"Hi, Ronette. This is Kevin. Inga in IS asked me to call everyone and run a test on their computers. Do you have a moment?"

I didn't know many names at the company, but I did know Inga was head of IS. She was a Russian woman, prettier than I'd ever be, efficient and nice. "What do you need me to do?" I asked.

"Can you go to your web browser?"

"Sure." I clicked on the icon. "What next?"

"I need you to enter an IP address. It's probably cached already in your address bar and will come up when you start typing it in, but we need to make sure. Can you type in 126.36..."

When I started typing, no history pulled up, and I began to feel uncomfortable. What if this was a hacker? Typing in an address would be just like clicking on an unknown link. "Kevin," I said, "what's your last name?" I had put "Kevin" in the Shoretel address bar and pulled up all six Kevins who worked for Xtronical.

"It's Nutter. But I'm not in the directory yet. I just started this week and they haven't updated the system yet."

"Do you mind if I call you back in a few minutes? What's your number?"

"Ronette, it'll be easier if I call you back instead. Can I call you in five minutes?"

"Sure."

I hung up and immediately called Inga. There was no answer. I bit my lip. Who else could I call? Pulling up my email list, I started going through it, saw the name Nick, and remembered he was also in IS. I punched his number.

"Hi, Ronette, what can I do for you?"

"Some guy named Kevin says he's a new hire in IS and is working with Inga to do some testing. Do you know anything about it?"

"There's no one here named Kevin," Nick replied. "I'd know. Sounds like social engineering to me. Good catch."

I hung up, relieved but nervous. Was that a real hacker I'd just avoided? Competition was tough in computer gaming, so anything was possible. Then again, it could have been Xtronical just doing a test to see if I'd be stupid enough to let a hacker through. Either way, it was unsettling.

I took my last piece of celery out of a bag in my drawer and munched on it slowly. The rest of my Friday went well, thankfully, and by 4:30 I was ready to head home. Though our office was located in downtown Sacramento, I lived in the suburbs in my very first apartment since graduating from college.

Funny how so many jobs required you to have a college degree, even if the job had nothing to do with your major. The psychology courses might still come in handy someday if I was lucky.

I pulled my clothes off as soon as I entered the apartment and rubbed Lucy's head. My sweet, ginger-colored cat couldn't have cared less I'd come home. Then I headed for the shower. It was a big night for me, my fifth date with Splaine. Every time I heard his name, I thought of Ricky Ricardo demanding that his crazy wife "splaine" something to him.

Splaine was a BYU grad with an MBA in business and had just moved to Sacramento for his first real job, so we had the beginning of our careers in common. He was cute, with two dimpled cheeks, a dimpled chin, and a square jaw. He always looked freshly shaven, though I wasn't crazy about his mousy brown hair. I still had freckles I tried to cover up with base, and no particularly appealing features, though my breasts were unnaturally large, almost embarrassing.

Splaine and I had gone to dinner a few times, gone to a couple of movies, and had taken one long walk through the park. While part of me found it exciting to date a good "catch," I'd heard Splaine yell one evening at a homeless person to get away from him, and once at church I'd seen him scowling at a young boy who was playing with his toy car just a little too loudly. I'd been smiling at the boy, imagining my own future son. It had taken me aback that Splaine found the boy annoying. After all, raising children was the whole point of the Church, wasn't it?

Still, dating was all about getting to know someone, and I certainly knew enough about the world to realize I was never going to find the perfect man.

At 7:00 on the dot, there was a knock at my door. I waited several seconds so as not to appear pathetically eager and then opened it. Splaine wore a tight knit beige polo shirt and khakis. "You look lovely tonight, Ronette," he said, handing me a single red rose. I had on a green dress, the sleeves woven in such a way you could see a hint of skin through the little swirls. I still hadn't gone through the temple yet, so I had no garments to cover. I hoped I wasn't being too daring.

"What excitement do you have in store for us this evening?" I asked, allowing Splaine to lean forward and give me a peck.

"How about a nice Italian dinner and then some shopping?"

"Shopping?" I laughed.

"Don't women like shopping?"

"I suppose," I said, still laughing.

"Just want you to know I'm all for it."

"How considerate."

Splaine's deep purple Camaro sat parked in the street. He held the passenger door open for me, and I stepped into the car. He turned on Beyoncé a little more loudly than necessary and we sped off. The hostess at Olive Garden led us to a booth next to the window, and Splaine allowed me to choose my seat first.

"How was your day?" he asked, picking up his menu and reading over the possibilities.

I made a face. "Mindy would never make a good Mormon. She asks for coffee every twenty minutes."

"Who's Mindy?"

"My boss." I talked about her every time Splaine and I met. Perhaps it was boring to talk about work. "How was *your* day?" I returned.

"Mark told me he liked my report," he said. "He promised he'd put me in charge of the next sales meeting. Pretty good, huh?"

"Yes," I said. "Impressive." The waitress brought some bread sticks to the table. I really wanted one but resisted. Splaine grabbed the top one and chomped down.

"Mmm," he said.

"Just like Italy?" I suggested. Splaine had served a mission to Milan several years earlier.

"Better," he said.

"Do you find the Olive Garden is like real Italian cooking?"

"There's a lot to be said for Americanization," Splaine replied. "We make everything better here."

I'd only been down to Mexico once, and while I wasn't sophisticated enough to distinguish real Mexican food from the fare at Taco Bell, it had been thrilling to be someplace where *everybody* ate Mexican. It made me feel worldly.

"I heard American pizza is different from Italian, too," I said.

"It is," Splaine agreed. "American's better."

I ordered chicken parmesan but only ate the chicken, leaving most of the pasta on the plate. Splaine asked if he could finish it while I worked on the rest of my salad. I was just finishing my last bite when the waitress came back. "Anything for dessert this evening?" she asked with a big smile.

"Actually," Splaine said, leaning toward her conspiratorially, "Derek said you could get us some zeppoli on the house."

The waitress frowned. "Derek said that?"

Splaine nodded.

The waitress forced a big smile again. "Be back in a minute."

"Who's Derek?" I asked.

Splaine laughed. "I called up before we came and asked who the manager was tonight. Then I asked for the name of the off-duty manager."

"And they told you?"

"Yep. And since Derek was off tonight, I knew I could use his name to get us some free dessert."

My mouth hung open. "You can't be serious."

Splaine laughed again. "Life is all about maneuvering."

"Isn't the correct word 'stealing'?"

Splaine wrinkled his nose. "The waitress is just building up customer loyalty. It'll be good for their business."

The young woman brought over two orders of small Italian doughnuts dusted with powdered sugar, plus a ramekin of chocolate sauce. "Enjoy!" she said.

The doughnuts looked enticing, but under the best of circumstances I couldn't have allowed myself to eat more than one. Tonight, I just shook my head. "I wish you'd asked, Splaine. I'm full."

He chuckled. "Don't you worry. I can handle all of them."

I think my own nose wrinkled as he shoved down the last one, but I managed a smile as he paid the check. We walked out to the car, and I breathed in the autumn fragrance. The air smelled so fresh I just wanted to take another long walk as we had a couple of dates ago.

"How about a stroll in the park?" I asked as Splaine held the car door open.

"How about window shopping downtown?" he countered.

"But we're not downtown."

"Well, how about the mall?"

I forced another smile.

The mall was pleasant enough, lively, with lots of people walking about. Somehow, though, I was reminded of the plastic ficus tree in our office. Life here seemed somehow artificial. Splaine held my hand, though, and I felt a warm glow. Maybe this venture wouldn't be so bad.

We stopped briefly in front of Barnes and Noble, then again in front of Banana Republic, though Splaine feigned indifference to the Victoria's Secret display the next window over. At a store called The Game Stop, he paused and said, "Ah, this is where your expertise comes in." He pulled me inside the store and walked over to a row of computer games.

"I don't know anything about games, Splaine."

"But you work at a gaming company."

"Sure do."

"Let's take just a few minutes to look through them." He then spent the next twenty-five minutes thumbing through an endless assortment of military and zombie and intergalactic games, reading the covers and admiring the pictures. Every few minutes, he would look over at me and smile.

It didn't take a psychology major to figure out that Splaine was still very much a little boy. That was fine for little boys, but not so great for husbands.

Finally, it was time to go home, and Splaine played more Beyoncé on the drive back. He got out and walked me to my door. As he leaned in for a kiss, I held up my hand. "I don't think this is going to work out," I said as gently as I could.

Splaine smiled, as if thinking I was teasing, and then his eyes widened. After a long moment of stunned silence, during which I started nonchalantly looking for my key, his eyebrows furrowed. To my horror, he got down on his knees.

"What are you doing?" I asked, fumbling around now in my purse for that key.

"Ronette, will you marry me?"

"What!?"

He took my hand away from my purse. "I wasn't going to say anything, but I had a dream about you last night."

I'll bet he did, I thought. And had to change his garments in the morning.

"The Lord told me you were the woman I should take as a wife." He stared at me intently, his expression dead serious.

"But—"

"The Lord told me," he repeated. After a moment, he added, "You know I was a senior zone leader on my mission. And I'm Elders' quorum president now."

"Yeah?"

"The Lord told me," he said yet again.

"Well," I said unhappily, taking my hand out of his grasp, "I'll pray about it."

He showed his dimples as he got back to his feet. "That's great," he said. "Just remember that I'm the priesthood holder and the future head of our family."

"Yeah?" I said again.

"So the Lord will probably be speaking most often to me."

I scrambled again for my key, found it, and slipped through the door, shutting it behind me. I turned the deadbolt and slid the chain in place. Then I threw my purse on a chair and shivered, hugging myself. I felt dirty.

But what if Splaine had been telling the truth? Joseph was the one who received hundreds of revelations, not Emma. The apostles today received inspiration for leading the Church, not their wives. I hurried to the bedroom, slipped out of my dress, and put on a nightgown. Then I dropped to my knees beside my bed and prayed.

"Oh, dear Heavenly Father, you don't want me with that man, do you?" I prayed for almost twenty minutes, but I never felt any kind of answer, other than my own unhappiness.

Thankfully, when I crawled into bed a few minutes later, Lucy curled up next to me. I put my face in her fur, so grateful she was there. She purred, and I was eventually able to fall asleep.

Saturday was a "special day," the day to "get ready for Sunday." I'd always loved that hymn. I did my laundry, vacuumed and mopped the apartment, and then cooked some vegetables and chopped up some fruit. I knew lots of Mormons ate their biggest meal on Sunday, but that had always felt like "work" to me, so I prepared my Sunday meal on Saturday. I also prepared my lesson for the four-year-olds I taught in church. If I didn't want the class to be chaotic, I always came prepared.

But throughout the day, Splaine's words kept coming back to haunt me. What if he were telling the truth? I knew we were all here in this life to grow. Even if Splaine wasn't the man I wanted him to be right now, perhaps he would be in ten years or twelve.

He said the Lord told him.

Late in the afternoon, after I returned from grocery shopping, I took out my scriptures and read some of the Book of Mormon. Then I knelt beside my bed and prayed.

Nothing, other than my own misgivings.

But I knew that services on Sunday would lift my spirits. I wore a bright blue dress and arrived ten minutes early. Although I felt obligated to sit with Splaine during Sacrament meeting, I was thankfully able to escape when I taught my class. The bishop caught me in the hallway afterwards. "Ronette, do you have a moment?" he asked with a smile. "I'd like to see you in my office."

Had Splaine said something? Was the bishop going to try to talk me into marrying this man? Damn, I had almost been able to slip into the parking lot unseen by Splaine and get away. I followed the bishop to his office and sat down as he shut the door.

"How have you been, Ronette?" he asked, his voice booming. "How's life after college? How's the job?"

"Fine," I mumbled. "Everything's fine."

"Meet anyone interesting lately?" His smile seemed more of a smirk.

"I'm always open to finding the right man," I said through tight lips.

"Wonderful," he said. "Wonderful. You don't want to miss out on motherhood just for a mediocre career."

"No, Bishop."

"So let's get down to business. I hear you've been doing great things with the four-year-olds."

"Thank you."

"How long have you been teaching them now?"

"Almost two years."

The bishop laughed. "That's enough to drive anyone crazy. That's why the Lord has called you to a new position."

I sat up. I hadn't been expecting this. "I like the four-year-olds," I said.

"Of course you do. But what the Lord wants you to do now is teach early morning Seminary."

My mouth fell open. I'd always hated Seminary classes when I was a teenager and had thought when I graduated high school I'd finally escaped them forever. I'd never been much of a morning person and getting to work for 9:00 was enough of a challenge. Back in college, I'd quickly learned never to schedule a class before 10:00. Getting into college in the first place had been difficult because my grades were so low in the first class of the day every year for four years in high school.

"Early morning…" I managed to say.

"You were great with the younger kids," the bishop went on. "And it's wonderful you had that experience to help prepare you for when you have your own children. But you'll have teenagers one day, too, so you need to be prepared for that as well."

"Early morning…" I said again.

The bishop laughed. "Well, you pray about it," he said. "But remember, it's not *me* calling you to this position. It's *the Lord.*"

I walked out of the office in a daze. Splaine was nowhere to be seen in the lobby. Perhaps he thought I'd already left and had given up looking for me. I stumbled out to my car and sat behind the wheel. I'd always done everything my Church leaders had asked of me. They were the Lord's anointed. But could Heavenly Father want *two* awful things for me at the same time? I closed my eyes and prayed, but I felt nothing other than my own despair.

Back in my apartment, I heated up my pre-cooked veggies and ate them slowly along with a Diet Sprite. I rubbed Lucy's head absentmindedly, barely aware of her purring. It was so awful being a woman. Why did God only speak to men? Even people like Joan of Arc were probably mentally ill. We never got to hear directly what Heavenly

Father wanted us to do. We always had to rely on what other people closer to him had to say. It wasn't fair.

I turned my head so I could look out the window. Such a peaceful, lovely Sunday. I prayed, letting Heavenly Father know of at least ten things I was grateful for over the past week, a prayer I made every Sunday. I was grateful I'd lost a pound. I was grateful Mindy at work had bragged about me in front of her boss. I was grateful my younger brother was doing well on his mission to Alaska. I kept reviewing the week, had already come up with twelve things, and was about to wrap up when I remembered the social engineering incident on Friday. "Thank you, Heavenly Father, for helping me not fall prey." That had been a close call.

Then I turned to my "however" list, things I needed help with. Only two items had made the list this week.

"Heavenly Father, do you really want me to teach early morning Seminary before work every day?" I asked. "And do you *really* want me to marry Splaine?"

I picked up my scriptures but was tired of letting other people tell me what God wanted of me.

I sighed and stood up. Lucy stretched and walked away. I knew jeans weren't appropriate attire for the Sabbath, but I put them on and drove over to the park. To walk surrounded by nature felt like an appropriate way to spend the afternoon. But it was hard to relax, thinking about Splaine. And my new calling.

What I really wanted to do was say no to the bishop. As much as I liked young children, and as much as I even enjoyed teenagers like my sister Karen, the kind of volunteer work I knew I'd truly enjoy was working for the Sierra Club once a week, not teaching youngsters. The kind of man I wanted to marry was someone who'd defend the poor, maybe literally as a public defender, someone I could look up to and be proud of, no matter how little money he brought home.

I sat on a bench, autumn sunlight filtering through a still leafy tree overhead, and looked out over the pond. There were a few ducks on the water, talking amongst themselves. One dipped his head below the surface.

Out of the corner of my eye, I saw someone approaching, and I casually turned to look. It was a man about forty, a couple of days' worth of stubble on his face, with a little dirt smudged on his shirt. I started to stand up.

"Oh, don't leave," the man said, tucking his shirt in where it was a little puckered. "Your father sent me to talk to you."

"My father?" I asked in surprise.

"Yes. He's a good man."

I nodded slowly. "Why did he want you to talk to me?"

The man smiled, revealing a broken tooth. "He said you have a good heart and could help me out."

"You need money?"

"He said you could lend me twenty dollars. You can call him if you like. He'll tell you."

"Why didn't he give you the twenty dollars himself?"

The man smiled again. "Oh, you know your father. He always wants to teach his kids a lesson."

This time I smiled. "Well, you sure have him pegged there. When did you talk to him?"

"Oh, just a little while ago."

"And do you often talk to ghosts?"

The man frowned. "Huh?"

"My father's been dead almost two and a half years."

The man stood up and stalked off, turning his head to glare back at me. He called me a bad name that no woman likes to hear. "Leading me on like that," he muttered. He walked a little further on and turned back once more. "Bitch."

As I watched him walk off, I felt impressed. He didn't go for spare change or even the minimal dollar. He went for the big bucks. And he had a pretty good story. Why he couldn't afford to wash his clothes once in a while I didn't know.

I looked back out over the pond. Two of the ducks seemed to be quarreling, but one swam off quickly and the other didn't follow.

I needed to do something to lift my spirits. Even atone somehow for something. I walked back to my car and drove a mile over to the Olive Garden. The waitress who'd served us the evening before wasn't there. "Could I speak to the manager?" I asked one of the other servers. He frowned, as if he expected me to file a complaint. But soon a young man around my age walked over. He had auburn hair, my favorite.

"Can I help you?" he asked.

"Are you Derek?" I began.

"Yes," he said uncertainly.

"Last night, my…boyfriend treated me to dinner here…"

"Was there a problem?"

I shook my head. "Well, because of what happened, he's now my ex-boyfriend. He cheated the server out of two orders of zeppoli. Said you'd okayed it."

A look of comprehension flooded his face. He nodded.

"I'd like to pay you back for that."

"Thank you. Otherwise, we'd have to take it out of Susie's pay. I'd hate to do it. She's one of our best workers."

We took care of the transaction, and as I was about to leave, Derek touched my elbow. "Not many people would have come back," he said. "Thanks."

"I don't like being made an accessory to…to…jerkiness."

He laughed. "Such a vocabulary. English major?"

I laughed as well. "Psychology."

He nodded. "I'm History. Almost as useful. Though I hear it's a good background for law school."

I turned to leave again, but Derek touched my elbow a second time before pulling back.

"Yes?"

"Would you like to go out sometime? I have Tuesday and Friday nights off."

Without being obvious about it, I looked him over. He wasn't very muscular, but then, he wasn't overweight, either. That alone had to say something for someone who worked at a restaurant. "What was the last charity you gave to?" I asked.

His eyes widened a little. Perhaps my question surprised or amused him. "To be honest, I don't have much money to give. But I did go to the park on my last day off and pick up trash."

"You like the park?"

"Love it."

Not a Mormon, I thought. At least, not an active one, since I'd never seen him before. But maybe a good guy. I nodded. "Tuesday won't work," I said, "but I'm free next Friday evening."

He grinned.

I took the paper he handed me and wrote down my number. "Let's go out for Mexican," I said.

Called to Condemn

"So, Russell, what do you think?" Bishop Hamilton asked, peering at me from behind his desk. "Are you willing to accept the Lord's call to serve?"

I looked back at the bishop, confused. I'd served as a missionary in Scotland for two years as expected. Upon returning to Seattle and enrolling at the University of Washington, I'd accepted a calling as Sunday School teacher for the fourteen- and fifteen-year-olds. That had lasted three years, until my graduation. After I began my MA program in English literature, I was called to be second counselor in the Elders' Quorum, where I also taught Priesthood lessons twice a month. That was my current calling.

Those types of callings I understood. My father had been first counselor in the stake presidency when I was in high school. My mother had served in the Relief Society. My sister Gretchen was serving in the Primary right now. It was a given that Mormons led a life of service. When the bishop called you—when the *Lord* called you—you accepted and did what you needed to do.

But this?

"I don't know, Bishop," I said slowly. "I'll have to think about it."

"*Think* about it?" Bishop Hamilton asked as if talking to a five-year-old. "Or *pray* about it?"

"I need to do both, Bishop."

He leaned back in his chair and touched the tips of his fingers together as if enclosing an invisible softball. His brows furrowed, and he frowned. "I just don't understand, Russell," he said. "You're one of our best members. Stalwart. Strong. That's why the Lord is giving you this special assignment. And you being an English major, it's perfect for you."

I wasn't quite sure how to put my concerns into words. English major or not, I was speechless. "It just seems so—so sneaky," I mumbled.

"The scriptures tell us to be as cunning as foxes to fight the evil in this world. Your father was in the stake presidency. Surely, you're aware we keep close tabs on members who are straying." He looked at me intently. "We have one of the high priests do a stakeout to see if a sister is having an affair. We have an elder from the Elders' Quorum follow a married man to see if he goes to a gay bar. We have people read all the anti-Mormon blogs to get information on people. We read the Mormon blogs, too. We have someone monitor Amazon to see when new books about Mormons are being written." He held out his hands.

"And that's where I come in."

"Exactly."

I took a deep breath and tried to accept the inevitable. "But you don't want me to actually read these books on the list," I said, holding up the paper he'd handed me earlier.

"Heavens, no!" The bishop laughed. "Satan is cunning, too. You don't want to get sucked into apostasy. You just need to write reviews on Amazon for the six books on the list, persuade other Mormons not to read them. Heavenly Father needs you to help protect his flock."

"Well, what's one little review going to do?" I asked, shrugging.

Bishop Hamilton laughed again. "The Lord doesn't put all his eggs in one basket, young man. There are several bishops having this same conversation with other saints across the country right at this very moment. Together, we can destroy any chance evil 'authors' have of dragging others to Outer Darkness with them."

The bishop looked at me intently again. My eyes dropped to the paper in my hand.

"Will you do the Lord's will, Russell?" he asked. "Will you accept your calling as Member Security Officer?"

"Isn't—isn't it lying to write a bad review without even reading the book?" I asked.

Now the bishop started to look angry. "We're *telling* you the books are bad," he said firmly. "So now you *know* they are. It isn't a lie to follow your leaders."

I sighed again. Interviews with bishops and stake presidents were supposed to be confidential, but I knew that Bishop Hamilton had told my father I'd confessed to masturbation, because my father had come to my apartment to have a serious man-to-man talk with me, asking me to join the Sons of Helaman support group.

If I didn't agree to the bishop's request now, he'd report me again, and the relationship with my father was strained enough as it was, first, because I hadn't wanted to go to Brigham Young University, and second, because I was in no hurry to marry.

There were third and fourth and fifth reasons, too. I didn't need to add a sixth.

"Okay, Bishop," I said, nodding. "I'll do it."

"The Lord will bless you, Russell." He reached over and shook my hand, and then I turned around to leave.

I drove back to my apartment slowly, looking at all the other young adults on the streets in the University district. Even in the cool spring weather, the girls wore sleeveless tops. Tight tops. Both they and the boys they hung out with were smoking and laughing. Probably on their way to drink beer somewhere as well.

The college years were hard on young Mormons. So many of us finally had full access to the Internet for the first time. We were learning uncomfortable truths in class, lies about the Church online. If I could save just a few of the others by writing these reviews, it seemed the least I could do.

Be as cunning as foxes.

I walked up the stairs to my second-floor apartment and unlocked the door. *Tess of the D'Urbervilles* lay on my coffee table. I really enjoyed 19th century British literature, from Jane Austen to Charles Dickens to Wilkie Collins to Thomas Hardy to Sir Arthur Conan Doyle to the Bronte sisters and most of the others as well. The problem was finding time to read everything. When one took a poetry class, most of the poems were relatively short, but when one specialized in fiction, the reading load was almost too heavy to bear.

And now I had to read these six additional books.

Well, I *didn't* have to read them. That was the whole point. All I had to do was write a few lines, maybe a short paragraph, about each book. I was used to writing a fifteen- or twenty-page research paper every week or two. I could certainly muster six paragraphs.

I turned on my computer and went to Amazon. I looked at the list the bishop had given me and typed in the first title. *Secret Combinations*. I read the blurb. It seemed to be about Mormons spying on each other.

I felt uncomfortable.

I typed in the second title. *Court of Love*. This one was about a vindictive bishop who sets out to excommunicate a young woman who refuses to stop talking about wanting to hold the priesthood.

The Unholy of Holies was about secret, evil rituals that went on behind closed doors in the temple by the leaders of the Church.

The bishop was right. This crap deserved whatever scathing words I could think of. And it looked like most of these books were self-published. They were probably awful even apart from their content.

The Pro-Anti-Nephi-Lehies simply made fun of anyone who believed the Book of Mormon was true. *Vampires of the Blood Atonement* brought up the lie that the Church used to kill apostates by shedding their blood to save their souls. But it did it in a supposedly humorous way so it wouldn't seem like the author was being as venomous as he actually was.

Finally, the last book was *The Tyranny of Silence*. I started to read the blurb, hoping to gather enough information to jot down some ideas for my review. But I was drawn back to the cover on the left side of the screen. The front showed a woman's face, Photoshopped so that her mouth was missing. There was a button on the Amazon page that let me flip to the back cover, which showed the lower half of a man's face, with a heavy five o'clock shadow, the man's lips sewn together with thick, crisscrossing thread.

I was angry. The Church didn't try to keep people silent, I thought. If anything, Mormons talked too much. Like the bishop blabbing my sins to my father every chance he got.

I turned back to the blurb. This was the story of a young married couple who discover truths online about the Church that the Church tried to keep hidden. When they begin asking questions in Gospel Doctrine class, they're called in to see the bishop, who tells them they'll be disciplined if they continue to make other members doubt.

When the bishop monitors their library cards through a member who works for the public library and learns the two are reading damning history books about the early Church, he disfellowships them, dismissing them from all their callings and not letting them speak up in class or in Sacrament meeting. Finally, the couple begin spying on the bishop and end up going public with the scandals they find out about him.

These writers must have lost their souls, I thought. Maybe they'd literally sold those souls to Satan in order to publish, thinking they'd become rich and famous.

My reviews could help nip that dream in the bud.

Though I had to admit, I'd occasionally had the same fantasy about my own bishop. Surely, he had some secrets he wouldn't want blabbed to *his* family members.

Thank goodness I'd never confessed my darkest secret, that not only did I enjoy 19th century British lit, but that I also enjoyed written porn of the period. I'd read *The Romance of Lust* three times already. Sometimes, I even fantasized about slipping a copy into the bishop's briefcase and then tipping off Sister Hamilton anonymously.

The Sons of Helaman was not helping me nearly enough. I looked back at the computer. This special calling was a blessing. It provided the chance to make up for so many of my awful sins. If I could help other people avoid sin, perhaps the Lord would be more willing to forgive my own.

And I could be blistering. Academia had certainly taught me that. I could skewer these six authors and make them regret ever putting pen to paper in an attempt to discredit the Church.

Murder was a sin, but killing in self-defense or during war wasn't. Being cruel to these apostates was no crueler than killing a Nazi was back in the day. And there was no doubt there was a war between good and evil here in the Last Days. This drivel proved it.

I was going to be good.

I reread the blurb and started writing down notes and ideas for my review, grateful now the bishop had called me to his office. He knew this was going to help me become stronger. The *Lord* knew. Maybe I'd even give up masturbating tonight when I went to bed.

I might be able to share this technique with others from the Sons of Helaman, get them to input some reviews as well. I supposed the call really needed to come from the bishop, but we were always told to be "anxiously engaged in a good cause." And it was a support group, after all. If I could offer support, I was going to do it. That would make me stronger as well.

And maybe the damn bishop would finally stop tattling on me to my father.

I looked again at the image of the front cover, the woman's face without the mouth. I flipped again to the back and looked at the man with his mouth sewn shut.

Then I read the blurb one more time.

The print book cost $12.95, but the eBook was only $1.99. Seemed the author was mostly interested in seeing that his book was read, not in making money. Financial greed wasn't the only kind of greed out there, of course. Greed for the souls of men was even more wicked.

But the book kind of sounded interesting. I would never really spy on my bishop, but it might be fun to read about someone else doing it.

Russell, you don't have time for this nonsense, I told myself. You have two more hours of homework tonight that absolutely have to be done. Get a grip.

I looked at the woman's face again, and I felt a small stirring in my groin.

I turned to look toward *Tess* lying on the coffee table and sighed. Then I pulled out my debit card and downloaded the abominable text. I could get even more ammo for my review if I read at least a few chapters, I thought. Specifics always carried more weight.

I turned on my eBook reader and began to read.

The Suicide Police

Miranda was almost at her wit's end. After the Suicide Police got her fired from West Jefferson hospital, she was never going to be able to pay her rent. It was the last day of April, and if she was lucky, her final paycheck—due any minute now—would be enough to cover the rest of her April rent. But then she'd never be able to pay her May rent, due tomorrow. What was she going to do?

She'd known for a while about the Suicide Police. They followed her from job to job, telling her employers all sorts of lies to get her fired. That's why they were called the Suicide Police, because they hounded you until your only option was suicide.

Miranda would have liked to fight back, to attack all these people ruining her life, but the truth was, she couldn't hurt a fly.

They sure had no problem hurting her, though.

Technically, she'd been fired from her job admitting patients in the emergency room for "poor job performance," but she couldn't help it if she couldn't type anymore. All the stress was too much to handle. The missionary in the library had told her that the Mormon Church wanted their money back from the three times they'd helped with the rent over the past few years. He'd threatened they'd start charging her

28% interest and ruining her credit. How could her boss expect her to function under those conditions?

Miranda closed all her blinds and took off her clothes. She needed a shower, but she wasn't going to give the police another opportunity to take a nude photo of her. She'd discovered that the police had had her under surveillance at every apartment she'd ever lived in over the past twenty-five years, always trying to catch a picture of her naked through the window.

She'd heard there were bounty hunters after a nude picture of her they could show in court to discredit her when her sex discrimination lawsuit against Tulane finally came up for trial. They'd pay a million dollars for a nude picture of Miranda.

She smiled. That was even more than people would pay for a nude picture of Marilyn Monroe. But it was still a bargain because it would save Tulane the many millions they'd otherwise have to pay her if they lost the lawsuit. Everyone calling her a slut and a whore was sexual discrimination, and they were going to pay for it!

The other nurses had told her there were lots of photos of her circulating on the internet, that it proved she was an exhibitionist. But she wasn't! If anyone ever saw her, it was because she'd had to open the blinds so her birds could see the sun. How could anyone blame her for that? What kind of horrible person would never let a poor little bird see the sky?

Still, there was that one security guard who'd said the police had a picture of her from when she still lived at her father's house, and she'd been walking on tippy toe. How could they know about that if they didn't really have the picture? She looked crazy walking on tippy toe, she knew, but she always had to walk on eggshells at her father's house because he yelled at her all the time. So it was mean to use that against her.

Miranda thought back for a moment to her childhood. At first, her parents had simply been neglectful. Her mother had diabetes, and emphysema, and Parkinson's disease and spent most of her time sitting at the kitchen table smoking. Miranda had had to climb chairs to get to the cabinets so she could feed herself even from the age of six.

Her mother used to lock her in the back yard every summer. One time, Miranda had begged to be let back in to get some water, and her mother had just told her, "Drink out of the water hose. And don't make a mess." Years later, when her father was teaching her how to drive, Miranda hadn't put her foot on the brake quickly enough, and her father had rammed his foot down on top of hers, breaking two bones.

Miranda stepped in the shower and felt the warm water run down her back. It was so soothing. Of course, she wouldn't be able to pay her electric bill, so she'd have no light and no hot water before long. But she was just going to have to live with it.

She'd already bounced several checks over the past few years. She couldn't help it. She'd been fired from six or seven jobs, and she obviously still had bills to pay, so she *had* to write the checks. Now she knew the D.A. was after her to put her in prison for thirty years. He was waiting to arrest her while she was testifying in court.

And she knew the apartment complex where she used to be a manager was also plotting against her. She'd learned that they'd put a camera in her apartment and taken pictures when Keith came over and had sex with her. They claimed she had sex in her office, to make her sound like a tramp, but her office *was* her apartment. The living room was the office, and the bedroom was behind folding doors. It wasn't *fair* to make her sound like a nymphomaniac. She'd only had sex maybe a dozen times in her whole life.

And the bishop was in on it, too. Miranda hadn't gone to church in ages, but the missionary had told her the bishop was going around telling people she lifted her dress in church and masturbated on the pews. *Why* would he say such things? Just to get her money when she won the lawsuit?

Everyone was trying to get her money. She'd even heard that Bonnie, the girl she shared a house with for three weeks twenty years ago, had been given $500,000 of her money. You just couldn't trust anyone.

Of course, she knew that even if she won her lawsuit, she wouldn't be legally allowed to keep the money. It turned out that after Hurricane Katrina when she'd gone outside to help a group of people taking care of abandoned cats, those people were *prisoners*, and so everyone who saw Miranda helping thought *she* was a prisoner, too. And no one who was a felon would be allowed to win a multi-million-dollar settlement.

Still, the moral victory would be enough.

That's what so irked her about the SPCA. They were accusing her of kicking a cat and breaking its ribs, when all she'd done was feed the cats selfish people had abandoned.

Even now, her apartment manager threatened her with eviction if she was caught feeding the strays again. But what kind of cold heart did it take to watch poor little helpless kittens starve?

Since the manager said he was going to have the SPCA arrest her, she had to be very, very careful around the cats and only feed them when she got home from work at midnight. She knew the Church had spy satellites tracking her, and she expected they'd be perfectly happy to cooperate with the manager.

After her shower, Miranda dressed again and went outside. It was hot, already 82 degrees even though it was still early spring, and still only 10:30 in the morning. She lived on Williams Boulevard in Kenner, just a couple of blocks from Lake Ponchartrain, so she decided to go on a walk. At least with all this extra time, she could finally lose a little weight.

Of course, with only two dollars left to her name, losing weight was probably not going to be much of a problem anymore. She hoped that check came today.

Miranda walked past the casino, wondering if she should take a dollar and try to win a million more. But she knew the city council had made a strict rule that she wasn't allowed inside. The rule was to keep her from winning money, but they couldn't legally tamper with the machines, so they simply had to bar her from entering at all.

Miranda remembered hearing about the woman who'd lost all her money and shot herself in the parking lot. And she remembered when the trail along the lake had been cut off with yellow tape because a nurse had injected herself with an overdose of drugs right at the water's edge when she had lost all her money, too.

Now the Suicide Police were hoping Miranda would do the same thing.

But she wouldn't. She'd show them. God would help her.

Miranda frowned. The truth was that God was a man, and all the men in her life had treated her poorly, even God. But she'd always heard that real blessings came after the trial of your faith, and there couldn't be a trial any bigger than this. The bishop had been as mean to her as any man, and he always pretended to be so holy. But the missionary in the library had told her the Church's defense was that Miranda was a sex addict, and they'd had to send Keith over once a month to knock her around and quench her sexual appetite.

Miranda strolled along, trying to exercise but also trying not to sweat. She didn't want to have to take another shower. Getting naked was always such a political risk.

Miranda stopped frequently and stared at the lake. There were tiny waves lapping at the shore, a couple of pieces of driftwood floating at the edge. A few dead fish bobbed in the water nearby, stinking up the air, and birds were darting along the wet mud, looking for bugs and anything else they could eat.

Despite the dead fish, it was a peaceful scene. Yet Miranda couldn't help remembering a story she'd read in her literature class in college, about a woman in Grand Isle who walked off into the Gulf to drown herself.

Those damned Suicide Police. Putting thoughts like that in her mind.

Well, it just proved that Miranda really had gone to college. Everyone at work kept saying she was a high school drop-out, and the Church went around telling everyone she was retarded and should be forced to wear an ankle bracelet to monitor her, but she had $40,000 in student loans to prove them wrong. She'd just gotten another call today from Sallie Mae demanding she start paying again.

She laughed.

Her voice made such a pretty sound in the stillness.

But Miranda quickly grew tired of the asphalt path and walked slowly back to her apartment complex. Just as she was arriving, she saw the mailman walk by, and he gave her a suspicious stare. What had he heard?

That look he had on his face. It was as if he was thinking, "Aha! They're going to sew up your vagina so you can't have sex with the other homeless people. Now you'll be sorry you didn't pay your tithing."

As if she would ever have sex with a homeless man!

Miranda hurried to her mailbox and unlocked it. There was her check. She ripped open the envelope and looked inside. $203.44.

It wasn't enough.

The manager was going to put an eviction notice on her door in the morning. It would be humiliating to be kicked out in the street, with all her gloating neighbors watching. If only she had some place to go right now. If only she had a friend.

She thought of Alice, her friend back in high school. They'd gotten along well and gossiped about the teachers and students and cheated off each other. But then one day, Alice stopped being her friend. It had all happened innocently enough. Miranda had a stomach pain that kept getting worse and worse.

Alice had suggested it might be appendicitis or a bleeding ulcer or worms inside her. Miranda had begun to moan in class and then cry out a little, and finally she'd begun screaming in agony as the pain grew worse. The teacher called an ambulance, Miranda was rushed to the hospital, and a cute doctor in the emergency room had examined her.

"Oh, for God's sake," he'd said in disgust. "You just have gas."

When Miranda told Alice about it, the girl had never spoken to her again. But Miranda had always wondered if maybe Alice hadn't poisoned her in the first place.

Miranda sighed. Life was so hard. Maybe it would be good if it was all over, if she didn't have to worry anymore. She walked over to her window, lifted the blinds, and then lifted the glass. She stepped over to her birdcage and opened its tiny door. "Go on," she said softly. "You can go now. You're free. Enjoy the world."

The one bird she still had left looked at her quizzically, stood at the edge of the door, and then flew into the room. It didn't take long for it to find the window and fly out. Miranda felt a stab of sadness but hoped the little creature would finally be happy.

Then she had a terrible thought.

"Oh, no, he's homeless now, too." She put her hand to her mouth, and her lips quivered.

But maybe he'd find true love and happiness, she thought. Maybe he would.

Miranda sat at her window and looked out at the apartment complex around her. Over there was where that man always leered at her. In that other apartment was the man who sometimes stole her underwear in the laundry room. And over there was where that horrible woman yelled at her kids all the time.

Miranda stared at the ground.

All she'd ever wanted in life was to be a mother. When she'd turned twenty-one, she treated herself to a parenting course. She'd liked it so much she'd taken another. And then one more. She was going to be the best mother in the world. You could overcome anything, she'd believed then, even an awful family.

The Church said family was the most important thing, and she wasn't going to let her parents ruin her future family. If she couldn't learn by example, she'd learn what to do in a class, and she'd still be a great mother.

Of course, she was pretty sure it would come naturally to her anyway, but she wanted to make sure. Something that important was worth the money those classes cost. God would see her dedication and reward her.

Then she'd had the miscarriage. That had been devastating enough, but it had never occurred to her she'd never be pregnant again in her whole entire life. How could that possibly be fair? What was God thinking?

But maybe God really did hate her. She'd always believed God was watching out for her that night the crazy guy crashed through the living room window while she was still living with her father. The gun hadn't gone off when the man put it to Miranda's head.

But Miranda now knew it wasn't just a random man on drugs. He was a hit man hired by the Church. Miranda had been accused of flashing the children in Primary class, and so she'd been marked for execution. It all made sense now. Her father had even been warned, so he could take out extra life insurance on Miranda, but he'd relented at the last minute and killed the growling man instead.

Maybe her father truly did love her.

She shook her head. He was probably just afraid of getting caught. These things always came out in the end.

Then a new thought came to her. Her horrible father had always told people Miranda had killed her mother, who had died of lung cancer while Miranda was at church one day. But maybe her father had killed the woman himself, just so he could blame Miranda.

It was amazing how clearly she could think, even at such a stressful moment as this. Why she could never pass her college math classes, she didn't know. It was probably just because she was out sick the entire two weeks her grade school class learned the multiplication tables. She'd never been able to catch up since.

Miranda looked in her fridge. There was one piece of bologna left, and two olives, plus an inch of milk in the carton. She sighed. Wrapping the bologna around the olives, Miranda took a bite of her "sandwich." If she was going to eat out of dumpsters from now on, she'd better stake out a spot near a good restaurant. She'd have to move her car every few days, or it would be towed, so she'd have to come up with enough money for gas.

Only bad people became homeless, though, and she'd always been good. Even those few times she had sex, she'd always confessed to the bishop. And it wasn't as if she *wouldn't* wait for marriage until she had sex. It was always the guys who insisted. What pigs. And how could Keith have been in cahoots with that awful bishop, when he didn't even believe in the Church himself?

Keith had been her soulmate. So why in the world had he married that other woman? And why did he have to go and die of Lou Gehrig's disease? She didn't even have hope anymore after that.

But maybe they'd be together in the Millennium. Maybe if she died now, they'd be together right away.

Miranda looked about her apartment and yawned. She was bored. There was nothing to do. She *liked* working. How was she going to fill her days now? Perhaps she'd go to the library and build her case against the police.

But why bother? Her shoulders sagged. *Everybody* was against her. What hope did she have to win any of her lawsuits? People just wanted to see her suffer.

But she *wouldn't* suffer. She wouldn't let herself.

Miranda got out two of her best bowls and grabbed the milk container. She went downstairs and set the bowls out where she usually fed the cats, and she poured the last of her milk. That hot sun would spoil the milk quickly, so she hoped the cats weren't far off.

"Here, kitty, kitty," she cooed, but when no cats showed up, she trudged back up to her apartment to throw the milk carton away.

Then Miranda got in her car and drove to the check cashing place down the street. They took 6% of her check, of course, but she'd have to live with it. It was the only check cashing place in the area she didn't owe money to for all the payday loans she hadn't paid back.

She kept $5 in cash but turned the rest into a money order. Then she drove a little further to the library and looked up cancer foundations. She found the Lung Cancer Alliance, wrote out the money order to them, and then begged a librarian for an envelope. The librarian had a stamp in her purse as well, and Miranda bought it for 44 cents. Then she asked the librarian to mail it for her. The woman gave Miranda an odd look, as if to say, "You think you can buy your way to heaven? You don't have nearly enough money."

But it was the best Miranda could do.

She was about to leave when she saw a three-year-old boy wandering alone. A woman who might be his mother was talking to a girl about four on the other side of the room. Miranda strolled over to the children's section, picked out an easy book with lots of pictures, and went up to the boy.

"How would you like me to read you a story?"

He nodded yes, and Miranda felt such an upwelling of love she almost couldn't speak. She put the boy on her lap, and for the next several minutes, she read the book aloud to him, using different voices for the various characters, and putting lots of emotion into the reading. The boy laughed and laughed.

"Come on, Raymond," said the woman then, extending her hand. The boy promptly ran over to her, and they walked off without another glance at Miranda.

But she still felt happy. She'd have made such a good mother. She knew it. And maybe in the Millennium, she could finally get pregnant again. She'd have her ovaries back by then anyway.

She'd have her ovaries now if that doctor hadn't lied and told her she needed a hysterectomy just so they could really do experiments on her eggs.

Maybe one of her eggs had been implanted in another woman, though, and Miranda had a baby out there somewhere in the world at this very minute.

She smiled at the thought and then went back to her car.

It was blisteringly hot, at least 86 or 87 degrees, and it wasn't even May yet. Miranda sat in her battered old car, which didn't have air conditioning, and was covered in sweat within seconds. But she had one more stop to make, so she turned on the ignition.

Burger King was just a few blocks away. It was her favorite of all the fast food places. Today, she ordered a Whopper, fries, and a large chocolate shake. It was her absolute favorite meal, one she could rarely eat because of the calories. But calories weren't an issue any longer.

Miranda stared out the window at a stray dog as she sucked up the last of the ice cream through her straw, and then she went back out to her car again. She looked at it sadly and then climbed in and drove to the stake center in Metairie. She'd gone to a lot of church dances in this building, she thought. She wondered if there would be a dance tonight. She hoped so.

Miranda had called the bishop just three days ago, swallowing her pride and asking for rent money one more time. But after he'd listened to her story, he had the gall to say she should commit herself to a mental hospital.

Miranda knew the Church was after her entire settlement, not just ten percent.

The bastards.

Miranda turned off her ignition, and with a deep sigh rolled up her windows. Within seconds, she was covered in sweat again. She reclined her seat and tried to get as comfortable as possible.

She thought about how happy Keith would be to see her again. But she wondered what her mother would say. And all the sick people she'd helped in the hospital who hadn't made it.

She hoped her little bird would be okay.

Then Miranda cleared her mind. She wanted to take a nap. It was never easy for her to fall asleep, she had such a strong mind, but she was tired now, so very tired, and she simply wanted not to think any more.

The high for today was supposed to be 88, Miranda thought. It must be nearly that now.

She longed for a drink of water, but she knew her mother wouldn't let her inside just yet.

She wondered if she'd be able to see her baby again, and raise him in the Millennium.

She wished she'd left a toilet full of feces for the apartment manager to find.

She hoped someone else would take care of the cats.

The heat was unbearable, oppressive, but Miranda felt herself starting to drift off into sleep. She felt so peaceful now, as if she were wrapped in a warm blanket.

She hoped the bishop would be the one to find her.

Miranda's hand moved in her lap, and she felt a little tingle. She'd never masturbated in her entire life, had never climaxed even once because Keith didn't care.

She began rubbing herself softly, and it felt good. She would have just one good orgasm before she died, she decided. She rubbed herself some more, but she was still feeling so terribly sleepy.

Finally, her hand stopped and her head turned ever so slightly as she began to snore.

The sun beat steadily down on the car, and Miranda began dreaming blissfully of a white wedding dress. And pink flowers. And smiling faces. The world could be such a happy place, she thought.

She woke up with a start, thinking she'd heard something. It was so suffocatingly hot, she rolled down her window and gulped in some fresh air.

They'd almost done it, she thought. Those Suicide Police had almost succeeded. But she was stronger than they were. She wasn't going to give in this easily.

Miranda needed a place where she could sleep all night. She turned on the ignition and drove over to East Jefferson hospital, where she'd worked three or four jobs ago. No one would notice her car in that huge parking lot, and she could go inside the cool air until nighttime.

She'd brought along her favorite two books and could start rereading one of them today, and then she could get new ones from the library. She'd spend so much time reading, maybe she could get an English degree online. She'd reinvent herself and make a life despite all those horrible people out there.

Miranda parked underneath a light pole so she could find her car easily after it grew dark. Then she picked up her book and shut the door.

She must look a mess, she thought then, all drenched in sweat. Maybe she should check her hair before going inside the hospital. There had been a couple of cute doctors here before who liked her. She didn't want to look homeless if she ran into them.

Miranda went to open her door to get her compact, and suddenly she stiffened as if she'd been electrocuted. Her keys were inside on the seat. She'd locked herself out of her car! And now she had no money to call Pop-a-Lock. She howled like a hurt cat, and an elderly couple passing by moved away.

Miranda cried for several minutes, pounding feebly against the side of the car, but then a new thought came into her head. Why, she'd simply get a security guard to open the door for her. While he was working on it, she could tell him all about the terrible things people were plotting against her. She could act flirtatious, maybe get him to offer to let her sleep over a night or two.

What was the worst that could happen? Perhaps one of her favorite doctors would see her with the guard and get jealous. Maybe she'd get a husband after all, even though she was already forty-nine. Why, perhaps fifty would be the beginning of the best part of her life. This could be the start of an exciting, brand-new adventure.

And without an address, the Mormon CIA agents on her trail would lose track of her before long.

Miranda stood up straight. Those stupid Suicide Police. They thought they could ruin her life. But Miranda still had plenty of life left in her. She couldn't be broken that easily.

She started off in search of a hospital guard. She wiped the sweat off her forehead, and she smiled.

How We Won Back Salt Lake

I'm from Logan, where almost everyone was Mormon, but after we grew up, my brother moved to Salt Lake and started a family, and my sister did as well. It was disconcerting to visit them and see so many women wearing sleeveless blouses, and so many men smoking. The capital of Zion was less than 40% Mormon now. What was the world coming to?

Then it happened. Work was getting slow in Logan, and my company transferred me to Salt Lake. I had to move with my wife and three teenage children, two in high school and one at the awkward age of thirteen, when every kid is a pain in the behind. We moved to Holladay, where at least the percentages were a little more in our favor, and tried to make a life in "the mission field."

Lorene, my oldest, was a senior in high school and had been transplanted well past the middle of her final year. "You're the head of this household," she told me after we arrived. "I know you're just following Heavenly Father's will. I'll be okay." She put on a brave smile, but I heard her crying every night in her room that first week.

Callen, my fifteen-year-old, couldn't have cared less. He played zombie computer games and collected zombie paraphernalia at any local Comic Cons we let him go to. He didn't have any friends to begin with, except two people he friended online, and would have been fine in the salt flats.

Brent, our thirteen-year-old, simply said, "I don't mind being bullied. It'll build my character, Dad." Then he smiled that sickeningly sarcastic smile that only thirteen-year-olds can muster.

Tina, my wife, said matter-of-factly, "I can make brownies for the non-Mormon neighbors. Missionary work always makes one feel involved. I remember writing to your nephew each week when he was on his mission to Japan."

I nodded, reflecting on Tina's dedication toward the one Gentile family on our block in Logan. She kept bringing brownies even after they insisted they weren't interested in the investigator's lessons. And even after they mentioned the wife was diabetic.

"I'll tell the bishop I want a calling," I said. "The brethren always appreciate a hard worker. I'll fit in in no time. And if I'm in good with the men in the ward, their wives and kids will be friendlier toward you guys, too."

Lorene was laughing at the dinner table three weeks later. She was pretty and vivacious, a blonde with a toothy smile, and two of the girls in her class had befriended her. Brent was more likely to be a bully than to be bullied by others, Tina was regularly bringing treats to the four neighbors on our block who weren't on the ward roster, and Callen didn't even seem to notice we were no longer in Logan. "How are things going at work, Don?" Tina asked as we ate her tuna casserole.

"Oh, fine, fine." My boss had deliberately spilled coffee on me twice this week.

"Tell me the truth, dear."

I shrugged. "Henry is on me every day. Nothing I do is ever good enough. He's not LDS."

Tina nodded. "It's a good missionary opportunity. He may be the whole reason we're here."

I ate another bite of casserole.

"Tomorrow's Friday, Dad," said Lorene. "Why don't you take your boss out to lunch? I treated Karrie and Noemi to lunch, and they like me just fine now."

"Why don't you give your boss Ex-lax brownies?" suggested Brent. "Then he'll go home early and you won't have to worry about him at all."

Callen tuned out of the entire conversation.

"Don," Tina said softly, "I think Lorene is right. You have to go the extra mile. That's the kind of act that draws the Spirit to us. And tomorrow is April 6. It's a special day."

I nodded. "At least there's no smoking in restaurants anymore. Henry's a big smoker. Cigars of all things. Ugh." Maybe it was Freudian. So many non-Mormons were gay.

The next morning around 11:00, I popped my head into the boss's office. "Can I treat you to lunch in a little while?"

Henry smirked, as if knowing I was brown-nosing him. I felt like…like…hmm, I wasn't quite sure I knew which scriptural characters were brown-nosers. I should probably read the Book of Mormon more than the minimum five minutes a day. "Sure. My favorite place is Benoit's. Is that okay?"

"Anything you like."

Back at my desk, I looked online for Benoit's. Just as I figured. Even lunch entrees were $40 apiece. He'd done that on purpose. Whatever. It'd be a good investment. I called Tina to let her know. "Now you be careful," she said. "No talk about the Church right away. It'll scare him off. Build up a friendship first. Don't say anything Churchy till dessert."

"We'll probably talk about work."

"No. This is to build friendship, not a working relationship. Ask him for some golf tips or something. Tell him it's Mormon Christmas and buy him a gift. Maybe something from Deseret Book."

Soon enough, it was 12:00, and I drove Henry to Benoit's in my car. We sat at a table next to the window, and our young server handed us our menus. I asked Henry about his family. He was divorced. I asked about his relationship with his kids. He had a six-year-old boy he saw two weeks each summer. I wasn't about to say anything disparaging. I also didn't say anything when Henry took a sip of his drink, a cocktail at this hour. Then I asked about his hobbies. He looked at me with a sneer and said, "I collect stamps. Want to come over and see them sometime?"

He sounded just like Brent.

We ate in silence for the next ten minutes. I kept looking at my watch and glancing out the window. It had been a windy day, with lots of dust in the air. Suddenly, I heard a crash and looked outside again. Two cars had collided not far from the restaurant. I watched as two men exited their vehicles. One was yelling, and the other looked strangely calm. They approached each other, and then the calm one grabbed the other man and took a bite out of his neck.

"Oh, my heck!" I shouted. "Did you see that?"

I turned toward Henry, but he had a glazed look on his face. He must have seen it, too, and was as shocked as I was. I stared out the window again, and now the "calm" man had the other on the ground and was continuing to chew on him. "Call 9-1-1!" I shouted.

There was lots of commotion in the restaurant, all due to people straining to see what had happened, I thought, but finally I realized there was something wrong inside as well. A woman screamed as a man thrust a knife into her hand at the next table. Two servers were fighting. A man was running out the door with his napkin still tucked into the top of his shirt. "Henry…" I began. But when I looked back at him, Henry's eyes almost appeared to have cataracts. He was reaching for me, and I bolted.

I dodged several other people on the street plodding around like mummies who'd just escaped their tombs, and I jumped into my car. There must be some kind of chemical leak in the area that was messing with people's minds, I thought. I drove away as quickly as I could, my windows up and my vent closed. I was so freaked out, however, that I didn't want to go back to the office. I pulled onto the freeway and headed straight for home. I took out my cell.

"Tina?"

"Don! Everyone's going crazy! Get home as fast as you can!"

"Are you all right? How about the kids?"

"I can't leave the house! Brent's already home. Said half the teachers at school went berserk. The kids all ran away."

What was going on?

I passed at least ten car accidents as I drove, my exit was almost blocked by another. I pulled into our driveway, and Lorene opened the door as I rushed up. She'd made it home safely, too. I hugged her and then kissed Tina. Brent was sitting on the stairs looking scared for the first time since he'd become an obnoxious tween. Then I saw Callen, calmly playing on his Xbox. "Callen," I said sternly. "At a time like this…"

There was a loud bang on the door, and we all stiffened. There was more banging, and then whoever it was walked away.

"It's zombies, Dad," Callen said, not looking up from his game. "It's the zombie apocalypse."

"Good grief, Callen."

"The TV says it's happening all over the Salt Lake valley." Tina grabbed my arm. "Do you think it's a terrorist act?"

"Could be." I saw someone run across our yard. "Let me close the shutters."

After I closed all the shutters on our downstairs windows, I went to our gun cabinet and unlocked it, handing out guns to Callen and Brent. After a moment's hesitation, I handed one to Tina and another to Lorene. Lorene had tears in her eyes. "It'll be okay, hon," I said.

"Too bad you don't have a machine gun," Callen said, his nose wrinkled.

"I hope someone tries to break in," said Brent with a wide grin. I think I liked him better scared.

"Let's go see if the TV has anything new," I said. We all huddled around the television. The channel showed a color bar with no sound. Tina switched to another station. A rerun of *Little House on the Prairie*. The next station had static. Tina switched one more time, and a terrified anchorwoman was screaming into the camera. Then the image was replaced once more by a color bar. We tried calling our relatives, but the cell phone lines were jammed with callers, and we couldn't get through.

"Can't you get a national channel?" asked Brent. "Jeez."

"Watch your language, son," I warned.

Tina finally got Fox on the television. A blonde anchor was shaking her head. "It looks like the Mormons have finally gone crazy," she said. "There are reports of widespread damage in downtown Salt Lake, and at least thirty-five people have been killed in rioting across the city. The numbers are expected to rise."

There were images taken by cell phones showing buildings being set on fire downtown, and people running back and forth in a frenzy. "At this point, it appears to be some kind of toxin. All air traffic has been halted in the region, and roads leading into and out of the city have been closed." We watched a while longer, but the reporters just kept repeating the same information. No one really knew anything.

The electricity and water were still on, but we ate an early dinner and kept the lights off once the sun set. We sat around the living room holding our guns in the dark, listening for the sound of anyone trying to break in. I stayed up all night keeping watch. There were screams and shouting and flickering lights. We kept quiet and prayed. Tina started to sing "How Great Thou Art," but I shushed her.

In the morning, I peeked out of an upstairs window. Two houses further down the block had burned down during the night. There were several bodies on lawns and in the street. One middle-aged man was gnawing on the arm of a dead teenage girl. I closed the curtain.

"No one goes outside," I said back down in the living room. "It's still going on out there."

"*What's* going on?" asked Lorene. "What in the world is happening?"

"It's the zombie apocalypse," Callen repeated. "It's just like that graphic novel."

We turned the news on low. So far, it seemed that most of the turmoil was limited to the Salt Lake valley. "We think the mountains surrounding the city are keeping the toxins localized," said one man who looked like a scientist. Soldiers and National Guardsmen in gas masks were riding throughout the city. Several of the gas masks had failed, and those men had gone crazy, too, so the military was pulling out for now.

Midway through the day, the electricity went out. "Let's get the generator," I said. I went to the basement and dragged the device upstairs. I'd bought one that ran on gasoline, but knowing that whatever emergency required us to use a generator might also limit our access to gas, I'd made sure the one I bought could be run on man-made energy.

I set up three stationary bicycles in the living room, and we all took turns riding to generate power. We also made sure to turn on the television for only a few minutes each hour, making sure nothing else was on in the house which might draw electricity other than the refrigerator. We had satellite, not cable, so that helped.

Thank goodness we didn't need air conditioning this early in the year.

The following day, the water went off. "Okay," I said, "no flushing if it's Number One, and if it's Number Two, still only flush if you're the second person."

"Oh, Dad, that's gross," said Lorene.

"You know we have a two-year supply of food," I said. We'd always been obedient to the Church on things like this. "But storing two years' worth of water simply isn't possible. We have enough for several months, but only if we're careful."

"Do you think this craziness will last two years?" Tina asked, her hand on her chest.

"I don't know," I said, pumping away on a bicycle. "The prophets have always said at some point we'd need our storage. This might be it."

"I always thought it was going to be because of an economic depression," Lorene said, pumping away on her bike.

"I always thought it was going to be because of nuclear war," Brent said, pumping away on his.

"It's the zombie apocalypse," said Callen, still playing with his damn Xbox. "They couldn't come right out and prophesy such a thing. That's why they've always been vague."

"Turn that thing off," I commanded. "We may need the batteries later."

Tina led us in a verse of "Count Your Blessings."

The next two weeks followed in much the same manner. We took turns riding the bicycles. We also took turns reading books to each other, getting through Dan Brown's *Inferno* and Walter Lord's *A Night to Remember*. We played Scrabble and chess and Monopoly and Uno. We held Family Home Evening as usual and held worship services on Sunday.

We used only the toilet located in the basement to keep the house from smelling too bad. Once every few days, I would bundle up the garbage in a sturdy bag and set it in the back yard against the fence. It wasn't easily visible from the street, so I hoped no one would be able to tell someone lived here. There were still occasional bangs on the door, at any hour of the day or night, and every day, we could see one or two more bodies in the streets. Another house burned down.

Even now, no one on the news seemed to know what was going on. There were more reports about areas near Salt Lake, but the vast majority of the trouble was still right in town. In some ways, the whole experience was liberating. I was getting to spend time with my family that I'd never been able to before. Callen was beginning to speak with us, and Brent wasn't being a jerk quite as often.

One afternoon around 3:00, there was a loud knock on the door. "It's Adam!" squealed Lorene, looking through the tiny glass window in the door just above eye level and blushing.

"Who's Adam?" I demanded.

"He's a boy in my class I like," Lorene answered. "He must be coming to check on me!"

"After all this time?" asked Brent, his lip curled.

Before I could stop her, Lorene ran and opened the door. Adam staggered into the room like a dead man. Lorene screamed.

"Shoot him!" said Brent.

"In the head, Dad," said Callen. "It's the only way to kill a zombie."

"He's got a can of beer in his hand," Tina said. "He isn't even a member of the Church!" She gave Lorene a dirty look. Then her eyes widened and she looked back at me. "Maybe this disease only attacks non-Mormons!"

"But he's a good boy!" said Lorene. "And the Johnsons down the street turned into these—these zombies. We saw them stagger by last week."

"They're jack-Mormons."

Adam was still plodding deeper into the house, his arms outstretched in a clichéd fashion. I reached for my gun.

"Well, ask him about the gospel," insisted Tina. She went up to the boy, who stopped and looked at her with his dead eyes. "What do you know about the Mormon Church?" she asked bravely. "Do you want to know more?"

Adam bared his teeth and lunged at Tina, and I pulled the trigger.

I dragged the boy's body out back and dumped him next to the trash. Lorene was crying when I came back in. "We shouldn't just wait in here hibernating," Callen said. "We should go out and try to kill all the zombies. Take back the city."

"No," I said. "The news is reporting that more of them are dropping dead on their own. We'll just wait it out. Heavenly Father had us prepare for two years. He did it for a reason. We'll be okay."

"Two years?" wailed Lorene. "That's forever."

"That's how long we have to go on missions," Brent reminded her.

"Yes, but missions are exciting," she protested. "They're fun. An adventure."

"Killing a zombie in our living room isn't an adventure?" asked Callen, smiling. "Let me shoot the next one, Dad."

"I think it's time we sang a hymn," said Tina. "How about 'Come, Come Ye Saints'?"

To appease the boys, I let them kill one zombie every couple of days, taking turns, of course, to teach them manners. By now, it was early May and the temperatures were starting to rise. We didn't have to worry about the smell from the basement bathroom, though, the smell from the back yard overpowering anything from inside the house. The national news still seemed to be flabbergasted at what was happening over here, but then one night, six weeks after this unspeakable ordeal began, NBC had some answers.

"It appears the terrible events in Salt Lake are the result of a virus that has been isolated in the brine shrimp from the Great Salt Lake, and in the bodies of those who have undergone this severe dementia. The virus seems to be present even in those unaffected by the disease. It looks like the actual dementia only takes place if the person infected has high levels of alcohol, nicotine, tannin, or THC in their bodies. A higher intake of gelatin from bone marrow seems to inhibit the disease."

"Oh, my heck," I said softly.

"The Church *is* true," breathed Tina.

"Unfortunately, this news comes too late for most of the victims, most of whom have died within a month of exposure."

We looked at each other. There were still occasional zombies on our street, I thought, and there shouldn't be if the reporter was right. Perhaps it was Mormons who were giving in to temptation and finally starting to drink alcohol because of the stress. The commandment was to "endure to the end." Heavenly Father had told us that for a reason. It looked like the weaker saints were being weeded out as well. Living in the end times was demanding.

Two more weeks passed before things began to return to normal. With the sick people no longer a threat, the rest of us started returning to work. The electricity came back on, as did the water. I was promoted in the office to take the place of a Gentile who'd died. Scientists poured into the city, and there was shortly a vaccine available, which was then manufactured for people all across the country, in case the virus spread.

The city's population was cut in half, but with an abundance of properties for sale at such low prices, people began rushing in from other states to scoop them up. I was happy to see that so many of them were Mormon. Salt Lake is now 81% LDS.

Lorene graduated late from high school and married a returned missionary. Brent is fourteen now and just as smart-alecky as ever. And Callen is back to playing on his Xbox around the clock.

Tina is now the homemaking leader and comes up with new ways to serve Jello every month.

I heard the Church is considering another monument next to the seagull monument, only brine shrimp don't make great sculptures. Still, the leaders are inspired. I'm sure they'll come up with something, even if it has to be tucked away in Gilgal Gardens.

It's great to live in Zion.

Polka Dots in the Chapel

It was time for the combined Relief Society/Young Women's conference, and the chapel was full of women from the age of twelve on up to ninety. There were probably two hundred of us sitting there. My thirteen-year-old daughter Nina and I found seats right in the middle of the room. This was a time we all came together to hear messages the Priesthood had for us as women. It was kind of like listening to a translator. We couldn't hear the message in the original language of maleness, so we had an interpreter tell us what God really expected of us.

"How long is this going to last?" Nina whispered as we opened our hymnals.

"Not too long. It'll be okay."

"You didn't answer my question."

I just smiled in return and started singing. Nina was at that age when she'd begun noticing boys. I'd heard her mention someone named Dirk to her friends. She wouldn't be able to date for another three years, and the anticipation was killing her. The last thing I wanted was to have Nina start kissing at thirteen, necking at fourteen, and then needing to wait several more years before she could take the next step.

I remembered my own teen years. There was no point in tormenting the girl. Making her wait until she was sixteen to start dating was kinder to her hormones than letting her start now. Still, the difference in rules at our house as compared to the rules in the homes of Nina's friends had started creating some distance between us. Nina no longer told me about her favorite songs. She no longer told me what jewelry she liked. She no longer talked about where she hoped we'd go on vacation. She simply seemed resigned to whatever her father and I told her on any given subject.

But no matter what we said to her, she didn't say much back. Only the minimum. I hoped our leaders would say something inspiring tonight to help Nina and all the other young women in attendance. Nothing about honoring one's parents, of course. That would slide right off their backs. But maybe something about the importance of communication in general. Something I could use later to start a conversation.

Sister Crowley offered the opening prayer, and then Bishop Carruthers began the meeting. He introduced the first speaker, Brother Wood from the High Council, who spoke about the importance of deferring to authority. That was important for men, of course, as well as women. Brother Thomason was next, speaking about the value of learning the arts of sewing and cooking. I thought it odd he hadn't asked his wife to address the topic instead.

Brother Kendall followed, telling us all about the necessity of having large families, especially urgent since so many non-Mormon women had stopped doing so, and those remaining spirits up in heaven still desperately needed bodies. So far, nothing we didn't already know, though I supposed it was always helpful reinforcing our beliefs. If Nina heard all this from an authority, she might accept it more than if it just seemed to come from me.

A couple more talks followed, these two at least by women. Nina was reading the hymnal, not really paying attention, but I figured she could get good information from the hymnal, too, so I didn't protest. At least she was here. Some of the sisters from Relief Society couldn't even get their daughters to come to church anymore at all.

Then Bishop Carruthers took the podium himself as the final speaker. One never knew if the good stuff was going to come in the first talk or the very last one. Since we hadn't heard anything all that interesting yet, I was hopeful for something now. The last lesson I wanted Nina to learn was that church was boring. Or more importantly, pointless.

"I have a serious message to convey to you all tonight," he began slowly, "a message straight from the First Presidency." He paused to let us absorb the gravity of what he was saying. "This message then is really direct from Heavenly Father."

We all straightened up in our pews slightly.

"It's about the importance of dress," the bishop went on.

I stared at him. *This* was news? That we were expected to dress chastely? I could feel a collective sigh of disappointment sweep across the room.

"You of course know not to wear skirts or dresses that are too short. Or to wear sleeveless or backless tops. Or anything too constricting. That all goes without saying."

So was there a new restriction, I wondered? Were we going to have to start wearing socks to cover our ankles? I was perturbed. I certainly wanted Nina to grow up with a respect for sexual morality, but I'd been hoping for something a little more meaningful. Then I felt a wave of guilt for allowing myself to think that chastity in dress wasn't a significant topic. I saw the way young girls dressed these days. Nina did need to hear this. Perhaps I did, too. You could never be warned against sin too much, what with all the secular influences everywhere around us telling us that sex was good. Sometimes, even I believed it.

Well, it *was* good, wasn't it? It was the basis of eternal relationships. I frowned. Or the cause of man's downfall. Or…I could still never really tell what to think. I looked down to make sure my breasts weren't too prominently displayed.

"It has come to the attention of the Prophet and his counselors that women today are drawing too much attention to their legs."

I looked at Nina, and Nina looked at me.

"It's of course acceptable to wear tights underneath your dresses in cold weather, but the problem is what *kind* of tights you choose to wear."

Several of the women around me looked at each other in confusion.

"For example, wearing white or black tights is acceptable. Something neutral. For a little girl wearing a pink dress, even pink tights might be okay. But…" The bishop looked out at the congregation uncomfortably.

Then to everyone's amazement, his wife, sitting three rows from the front of the chapel, spoke up. "Just *what* are you saying?" she said icily.

Now everyone was paying strict attention, even all the young girls looking forward with anticipation.

Bishop Carruthers continued. "The First Presidency wants us to convey that certain colors of tights are not appropriate." He paused and swallowed. "For instance, bright colors draw too much attention to the legs. As do stripes. And polka dots." Even from this distance I could tell he was sweating. "Anything 'loud' should be avoided."

"You mean, like my paisley tights?" Sister Carruthers said tartly. "Are you saying *my* clothes tonight are inappropriate?"

The bishop paused a long time, so long that everyone in the chapel grew uncomfortable. You could hear a pin drop. "Yes," he said finally. "Yes, your tights are inappropriate. They…they draw attention."

Though I couldn't see Sister Carruthers's face from where I sat, I could feel the intensity that must be gathering behind it. "Would you rather people were looking at my ass?" she replied, standing up and smacking her behind. "Or my breasts?" She clapped one hand on each breast.

The bishop looked down at his wife and then let his gaze cover the entire chapel before returning to his wife. He didn't look uncomfortable anymore. He looked determined. "Sister Carruthers," he said, "you women need to be *completely* chaste in your dress, not just *mostly* chaste."

Sister Carruthers waved her arms over her head in frustration. "I'm out of here!" She pushed past the others on her pew and stalked quickly out of the chapel. Everyone was horrified.

Except Nina. She was covering her mouth, trying not to giggle. I looked at her, her legs covered in bright green tights. Then I looked down the pew toward another young woman sitting with her friends. They all had on tights. Two of the girls were looking down at their legs in shame.

"Sisters," the bishop went on, trying to calm the murmuring that had started throughout the room, "this comes directly from Salt Lake. The Prophet himself has deemed this vital enough to address to you here tonight. This is a pressing matter."

Pressing, I thought? Paisley tights in the chapel?

Something shifted in my head.

I suddenly remembered when I was a teenager and my mother finally sat me down for "the talk." After vaguely explaining the details of sex, she put her hand on my arm and said softly, "Now, Crystal, you must be careful with this special power Heavenly Father has given you. It's the power to build a man up or ruin his life. You can be an inspiration or a temptress. You must always be attentive not to look too appealing, just enough to get a man to marry you at the right time, but even then you must be very, very careful, or your…" Now she whispered. "…sexuality…" Then she was back to her normal voice. "…can destroy your life as well as that of others."

I remembered feeling like a leper or tuberculosis patient from then on, someone with a disease lurking deep within me that I needed to be careful to keep in check and not spread. Any time I put on make-up or bought a particularly pretty outfit, I felt the shame of sexual weakness and impurity. It would be years before I realized the boys were given a corresponding sense of shame about masturbation. All these young lives taught to fear and loathe their sexuality instead of respecting and appreciating this gift from God.

Even today, knowing better, some of that feeling persisted. After Stephen and I made wonderful, tender love to each other every Sunday, I'd wash up afterward and pray, "Was that okay, Heavenly Father? Was that okay?" And we'd been married over fifteen years now.

I looked at Nina again. She was trying to compose herself, looking at me guiltily. The absurdity of the meeting struck me suddenly with full force. This was a girl living in the Last Days before the Apocalypse. What kind of challenges faced her on a regular basis? When she talked to me at all, she was telling me of some mean thing one or another classmate had done to someone else. Shouldn't there be a talk about not bullying, or how to help others who were being bullied?

Nina sometimes complained about wanting to watch television programs her friends were viewing that we wouldn't allow her to see. That was when she dared to say anything negative at all. Shouldn't there be a talk about how not to be Greek in the midst of Greek culture? Even the Jews taught that lesson every Hanukkah.

My daughter always stared at the news in horror when we watched as a family, though she never allowed us to know what she was thinking. Shouldn't there be a talk on how to work together as a family for positive change in the world?

"So tomorrow at Sacrament meeting," the bishop continued, "I hope to see all of you who choose to wear tights come wearing tights that are more appropriate in coloring than those which many of you wear tonight."

Nina still looked as if she wanted to laugh. I suppose that was good. But I didn't want to laugh. I wanted a message from the Prophet that wasn't petty. I wanted a message from God that told me he respected me as a person.

"We'll now sing the closing hymn, *I Need Thee Every Hour*, and then the closing prayer will be offered by Sister Clarkson."

I opened my hymnal again and sang the words without paying much attention. I didn't bow my head during the prayer, though, still in shock. I looked about at all the other bowed heads and felt an incredible urge to shout an obscenity. I looked up at Bishop Carruthers sitting on the podium, seemingly at ease again despite his wife's abrupt exit. And despite the unlikelihood of getting any nookie this weekend. I stuck out my tongue.

Then I realized that was as petty as his message had been. This attack called for a serious response.

Nina and I walked out to the parking lot along with everyone else after the meeting adjourned. As we buckled up in our seats, I turned to Nina. "What did you think?" I asked.

"It was okay." She shrugged noncommittally.

Her answer angered me. Not anger toward her but toward the men who made her afraid to speak her mind.

"It's only 8:00," I said. "The mall is open until 9:00. What say we go out and buy some new tights?"

"Oh. Okay."

"Bright red ones with electric blue polka dots," I added.

"Mom!"

"We want to wear our Sunday best tomorrow for services." If I'd learned anything at church, it was how to be passive-aggressive. I smiled, and after a hesitant moment, Nina smiled back. We pulled out of the lot and headed for Northgate mall. I turned the radio on low to a rock station I usually never permitted, and I looked over at Nina again. She still looked a little unsure of herself. I wondered what I could say to get her to open up about Dirk.

I decided just to ask.

Fannie Lou Soils Herself

It was July 25, blisteringly hot in Meridian. Fannie Lou looked out the screen door onto the porch. Two calico cats were sleeping lazily in the shade next to the swing. There was a wasp nest on the underside of the swing, so no one could use it until someone knocked the cursed thing off.

Not that there was anyone to use it. Fannie Lou hadn't sat on the swing in probably two years, not since Lester died. Her only daughter, Marsha, and her family lived in Memphis, only coming to visit once every other year on Christmas. Her son, Nathan, lived just five miles away and came by once a month. Tomorrow was her birthday, though, so Nathan was bound to make a special visit, even if his wife didn't stop by with him. His kids were grown and moved out and rarely stopped by, either.

Fannie Lou spent most of her day reading the newspaper. She'd read half in the afternoon after it came in the mail, and the other half the following morning while waiting for the next day's news. Other than that, she spent most of her time sitting on the sofa and looking out through the screen door. Sometimes, a chicken would walk by. She only had a few left. Raccoons or foxes or wild dogs had gotten the rest.

There was nothing to watch on television, nothing to do. It was hardly worth turning eighty, she thought. Why didn't the Lord simply take her? She was ready to go.

"Endure to the end." It was what the Church always taught. She'd been such a good girl all her life, a good Mormon in the evangelical Bible Belt where she was treated as if she weren't even Christian. Marsha had married a non-member and left the Church as soon as she turned eighteen.

Nathan had married another Mormon, but they'd stopped going to church by the time their firstborn was in kindergarten. That left just her and Lester on the path to the Celestial Kingdom, and it was a lonely path. The Church was all about family, but what would it be like to make it to the presence of God without your children or grandchildren in tow?

Fannie Lou had always thought if she lived long enough, she'd finally see her kids return to the fold. Now she was turning eighty, and there was no more hope today than when she was fifty. "Please, Heavenly Father, show me a sign," she prayed as she watched one of the cats absentmindedly swat at a fly that kept lighting on its nose. A rooster crowed somewhere behind the old barn.

It was hot and sticky in the house. Fannie Lou had never wanted an air conditioner. It made a person weak. The kids said that was why they never visited in the summer. And they never came in the winter because her only heat was the fireplace. The house had been built in the 1940's, a cute little house, even now.

There was a spot on the living room floor that looked like termite damage, but Fannie Lou couldn't afford to do anything about it. She'd only be around a few more years anyway. And no one wanted the house. What did it matter?

Fannie Lou looked at the clock on the mantel. Just past 1:00. The mailman should have passed by now. Maybe there was a birthday card waiting for her. Something other than junk mail and bills. Since Lester died, she hadn't been able to go to church. As a woman, she'd never learned to drive. Her Visiting Teachers came by every few months, but they were young women Fannie Lou didn't know, and their visits always seemed more about checking her off a list than really getting to know her.

Still, it was human contact. Her nearest neighbor, Betty Lee, who lived just a third of a mile away, stopped by once a week to bring her to the grocery. Her next nearest neighbor was a mile beyond that. It was nice of Betty Lee to help, but she always tried to get Fannie Lou to accept Jesus as her savior. She was being a *missionary* to Fannie Lou. It drove Fannie Lou crazy.

She pushed open the screen door and stepped out onto the porch. The wood along the front edge was splintered and decaying. Someone was going to trip on that one of these days. The left side of the porch behind the swing was sagging, looking as if it might fall off onto the ground at any moment. There were three more wasp nests along the roof. The wasps had that reddish tint to them that showed they were the bad kind.

Fannie Lou walked down the cement steps and crossed the yard. The grass needed mowing. Maybe she'd ask Betty Lee if her son could do it this weekend. Fannie Lou had seen a snake in the yard last week. She didn't get close enough to tell if it was a moccasin or just a king snake. She hated any kind of snake. Made her think of the devil in the temple film, a thought which made her wish she could go back to the temple once more before she died. The grass had grown up around the rusting Volkswagen Beetle, Lester's old car, a faded baby blue. The windshield was so dirty now she could hardly see into the car anymore.

She reached the gravel driveway and began walking. It was a good three hundred feet to the paved road where the mailbox was situated. It was surrounded by honeysuckle which always had more wasps flitting around. Fannie Lou listened to the birds chirping, the steady hum of insects in the woods to her left and the overgrown field on her right. Up high in the air, three buzzards circled slowly.

Fannie Lou sniffed the hot air. Whatever had died hadn't died very close by. That was a relief. There was a pack of wild dogs that roamed the area. People had thrown away dogs they no longer wanted and those dogs had united together to survive. Now they were no better than a pack of wolves. There were reports of young calves being killed. One boy nearby had been attacked, but his mother had driven the dogs away with a gun.

At least there'd been no bears or panthers spotted in the past few years. That was progress, wasn't it?

Sometimes, Fannie Lou missed country life the way it used to be back in the old days. Lazy days fishing in the creek. Blackberry picking in the summer. Now everyone just bought jam at the store. Frozen fish sticks in a box.

Fannie Lou was about halfway to the mailbox when a large grayish brown rabbit darted suddenly across the driveway. It so startled her that she stumbled and fell onto the gravel, tearing her pants and skinning her knee. Skinning her left hand, too. There was a pop and immediate searing pain.

She'd broken her hip.

Fannie Lou tried to get up, but the pain was excruciating. She just couldn't do it. She was right at the bend in the driveway, so no one could see her from the road. Not that anyone would have been looking anyway. What in the world was she going to do? "Heavenly Father, please help me."

It would be another day and a half before Nathan stopped by for her birthday. Would she have to lie here till then?

What choice did she have?

But fifteen minutes later, lying in the blazing sunshine, Fannie Lou knew she'd never last the rest of the afternoon in this unrelenting heat. She was going to have to do something. It was probably a little closer to crawl to the road than to the house, but there was no guarantee anyone would pass by anytime soon. Better to go back to the house and call for help.

She dug into the sandy gravel with her fingers and pulled herself around so that she was facing the house, every tiny movement like someone flaying the skin off her back. It felt as if someone were stabbing her. Burning her with cigarettes. Sweat was already pouring from her face, and she'd just begun.

Fannie Lou wasn't a strong woman, though she did still carry her own logs to the fireplace in the winter. She still caried her own groceries. She still fed the chickens. But pulling her body along the orange gravel was harder than any of those tasks. She had to cross a trail of ants at one point, and she could feel the stings as she inched along. At least it wasn't an entire bed of fire ants. That would probably have killed her.

"Heavenly Father," she prayed out loud, "is this the end? Have I finally made it?" She hoped to be taken home. She wanted to see Lester again. Maybe God had made her fall as a birthday present. All her trials might finally be over.

She stopped crawling and sighed. Perhaps she should just let the inevitable happen. No one could last six hours in this harsh, desert-like sunshine. It must be 95 today. And six hours of misery wasn't as bad as what Lester had had to endure with his bone cancer. She was getting off easy.

Fannie Lou wished she could have been a missionary in her younger days, done something exciting with her life, something one could never regret. But girls weren't going on missions back then. She could have gone to France or Norway or Japan. Maybe she should have moved to Salt Lake and married there. Her kids would surely have stayed in the Church then. Had she failed them by trying to stay and build up Zion out here?

Marsha and Nathan wouldn't even miss her. They'd feel all inconvenienced to have to come to her funeral, would be glad that would be the end of their visits. She'd be doing them a favor by dying. Doing them a favor and herself, too.

Fannie Lou blinked. The heat was unbearable. She could tell she was already beginning to burn. The ant bites burned and itched. Sweat kept running into her eyes. It stung.

And she really had to go to the bathroom. Why hadn't she gone before she left the house? She shook her head in disgust. It would be mortifying for someone to find her body after she'd soiled herself. She just couldn't have that. Maybe she'd better try to get back to the house after all. If Heavenly Father was kind, he'd still let her die in the hospital. Lots of people died in the hospital these days.

Fannie Lou dug her fingers into the gravel again and started pulling herself forward once more. She could hear rustling in the trees and bushes off to the side of the driveway. If it was the dogs, they'd have already come for her, but they still might not be far off. She didn't want to be eaten alive.

She looked up. At least the buzzards would wait till she was dead.

A grueling hour later, Fannie Lou reached the yard. Her clothes were ruined. Just thirty more feet to the front porch. She could do it. Her scrapes were probably so infected now she was doomed regardless. The idea was a relief. And the grass felt so soft and cool after the blazing gravel. If only she were in the shade. She might not mind dying then.

Fannie Lou dug her nails into the earth and pulled herself forward again. She felt a few more bites from random insects, probably more ants, and then halfway to the porch, she stopped dead still. The grass was moving ahead of her. She hoped whatever it was would go away.

But a moment later, she saw it. A snake, staring right at her. She didn't know what to do. Should she yell and beat the grass to scare it away? Maybe a snake bite wouldn't hurt too much. She'd die a lot quicker than she would from the heat.

It could still be a blessing from God. She stared at the snake for a full minute, and the snake stared back. Then it slowly slithered away.

Fannie Lou realized she'd wet herself. The warm liquid made her clothes clump annoyingly around her waist. How could she face the world after something like that? "Please, Heavenly Father, take me now."

She could feel she needed to relieve herself in another manner, too, one that would force Nathan to put her in a nursing home if he found her. She shook her head. Surely, Heavenly Father could manage to give her a heart attack. It would hardly take a miracle at her age. She tried to will herself to die.

"Endure to the end."

She *had* to fight. What would happen if she lived a good life for seventy-nine years, three hundred and sixty-three days, and then gave up on the last day? She'd lose out on the Celestial Kingdom. After all that effort. She *couldn't* give up.

Fannie Lou dug her fingers into the grass and inched forward, the sweat and dirt stinging her wounds. There was a big root from the tree in the front yard to pull herself over. She crawled across some fresh chicken droppings and heard barking in the distance. Multiple barks from multiple dogs.

But some of her neighbors owned more than one dog. It didn't necessarily mean the wild pack was anywhere around. The sun was still beating down, casting the tree's shadow in the other direction. A few flies flitted about her face, trying to drink her sweat. Even a wasp lit on her to get at the moisture. She stayed still so as not to anger it.

She could smell the urine. In this humidity, the dampness wouldn't dry for an hour or longer, despite the heat. She kept pulling herself forward and finally reached the steps, pausing to catch her breath. The barking wasn't quite so distant anymore. Maybe it was another neighbor's dogs.

"Don't let me be eaten alive," she prayed. "I've been good. Don't be a miserable bastard, Heavenly Father."

Fannie Lou bit her lip. How could she talk to God in that manner at a time like this?

The next few minutes were the worst of Fannie Lou's life. All the pain of the day was nothing compared to crawling up those three cement steps. Surely, the agony alone would kill her, she thought.

But it didn't. The jagged boards dug into her skin through her clothing, bruising her, nicking her, but she was finally on the porch. The cats looked at her and yawned. One of them came up to sniff her face for several moments and then trotted casually off the porch to go somewhere else where she wouldn't be disturbed. The other stared at her for a long moment, scratched behind its ear at a flea, and then licked her paw. A few wasps buzzed around but seemed to ignore her. A persistent fly kept landing on Fannie Lou's cheek.

"How much longer, Heavenly Father?" she asked. "Till I'm eighty-five? Ninety? When can I come home?" Her chest hurt from all the exertion, and for a brief moment, Fannie Lou thought she was having a heart attack, like her own mother had suffered all those years before.

She suddenly grew very dizzy, feeling her head spin in circles, and had a panic attack. Not a stroke! Please, dear Lord!

But the panic grew out of something else, other thoughts flooding her brain.

"What if none of it's true?" she thought desperately. "What if I've been wrong all these years?" She clawed frantically toward the edge of the screen door but couldn't quite reach it. "What if the Baptists were right? What if I'm going to Hell?"

Fannie Lou had never wanted to live so much in her life. She thrust herself forward with the last of her energy and grabbed the screen door. She yanked it open, and the cat scooted inside immediately before the opportunity was gone. Fannie Lou dragged herself into the house, sighing in relief when she heard the door flap shut behind her.

She was safe now. Only ten more feet to the phone.

The smell of the urine was stronger in the house. She wouldn't call Nathan or his wife. She'd call 9-1-1. The paramedics wouldn't tell on her.

Crawling on the floor wasn't as painful as being outside, but it was harder to get traction. Still, it was only a few minutes later before she reached the telephone. She dialed. "What is the nature of your emergency?" a monotone voice asked her. Fannie Lou explained, and the woman assured her in a bored manner that help was on the way.

She'd made it, she thought. She'd made it. She'd done her duty and not given up. Now it didn't matter if she died.

Only it did matter. Lester's death hadn't made her question things the way the possibility of her own was. She wondered if she should ask Betty Lee to take her to the Baptist church just down the road once she was able to walk again. Should she demand her Visiting Teachers drive miles out of their way to bring her to the Mormon church on the far side of town? She'd believed all these years. But believing wasn't the same thing as knowing. What if you believed something that wasn't true? What then happened on the Other Side? Surely, there was no consolation prize for those rooting for the wrong team.

Maybe she was only proving that she'd never been a true Latter-day Saint all those years. So many years. And ready to abandon her faith after one measly afternoon of tribulation. She shook her head. She was just pooping all over her own soul. She looked about worriedly, hoping no one had overhead her vulgar thoughts.

Fannie Lou's chest still hurt. Her bug bites burned and itched. She was still drenched in sweat, beginning to stink. She looked up toward the ceiling, her eyes narrowing.

What kind of a God treated an old woman like this?

Then she caught her breath. What if there was no God at *all*, she thought abruptly. A whole new world of possibilities flooded into her mind, none of them good. She put her hand on her chest and rubbed in small circles, waiting, waiting, waiting until she heard the sharp, comforting sound of the siren approaching slowly in the distance.

The Messiah of Tau Ceti

It was my job as the U.S. ambassador to the UN that first got me talking to Zigmo. My calling as a bishop a few years before had taught me the importance of tact and discretion, but it was my political connections that had landed me the job. The hardest thing about politics, I'd learned, was not to use one's position of power to abuse others. The temptation was always there, and I sometimes had an overwhelming urge to hurt people I didn't like. I hoped the arrival of this group of beings from Tau Ceti would usher in a reign of peace on the Earth. Despite our own best efforts, the UN hadn't managed it.

After the Tau Ceti leader addressed the General Assembly, a large group of us retired to the lunchroom, where the U.S. delegates jostled to produce "American" food as the first representative Earth meal. We were scheduled to serve hamburgers, but then the Indian delegation amended it to veggie burgers. I remember that Zigmo didn't like pickles.

There were plenty of other dignitaries for the aliens to mingle with. Most of the Tau Ceti delegation were talking to various leaders from the U.S. and China and Japan and Germany. But Zigmo looked a little depressed and kept to himself. And while everyone would just about have killed for the opportunity to talk to him, people were also a little intimidated, afraid. So when a delegate from the U.K. turned up her nose as Zigmo sat beside her, abandoning her meal and moving away, I saw my chance. I slipped into the vacated seat and offered my hand.

"Spencer Young," I said, smiling pleasantly. I hoped smiling was a sign of friendliness on their world. That it didn't hide the nastiness it sometimes did on ours.

"Zigmo Kitel Marti," he replied listlessly.

"Do you not feel well?" I asked. His lack of enthusiasm for meeting us rather irked me. I knew I sometimes felt contrary, but it seemed odd not to make more of an effort when first meeting the inhabitants of another planet.

"Oh, I'm fine." Zigmo had some kind of computerized translator hanging around his neck, like something out of *Star Trek*.

"Do you not like Earth?" I asked. "Have people been mean to you?" I thought of the prissy British woman, and I again hoped these beings were going to bring peace to our world. There had recently been a genocide in Tanzania, there was fighting in Afghanistan, and an office worker in Tulsa had just opened fire on his coworkers, killing seven.

I knew I had my own demons as well. Despite my attentiveness, my wife was often frigid, and though I tried to be patient and understanding, there were times she led me on and then changed her mind when I felt an incredible urge to simply force her into sex.

There were times when my fifteen-year-old son mouthed off to me in front of others that I wanted to bide my time and then smack him hard when we were alone. There were times when my sixteen-year-old daughter was dropped off at the house by her skuzzy boyfriend that I wanted to slip out and cut the brake line on his car before he left.

I suppose everyone had evil impulses once in a while. It was part of the fight between God and Satan for our souls. I wanted to be on God's team, and I forced myself to be good and respectable and decent. I truly believed in Mormonism, and I wanted to go to the Celestial Kingdom. Having faith is what made saints out of sinners. It's what had made me rise up the ranks and try to make a contribution to society.

Zigmo shook his head. "This is our eighteenth world in four years. Four years ago, before we discovered Kartak Drive, we were limited to our own solar system. But now, well, your world has changed today, but ours changed, too. Life isn't like it used to be."

I frowned. Why did he sound so unhappy? I'd been a fan of *Star Trek* and *Star Wars* and *Stargate* and any other show or movie that opened up other worlds to me, even if only in make-believe. I remembered the creators of *Star Trek* saying they'd chosen the human form as a model for the various aliens in their universe as a scientific principle, when it was clear to me it was all a matter of costuming and the actors' guild and make-up. Before computer graphics, how else were they going to depict aliens?

But what I found fascinating right from the moment these folks from Tau Ceti appeared was that they looked *exactly* like us. Their skin had an odd orange accent, like a Coppertone tan, but other than that, they could have been from France. Fox News claimed the arrival of the aliens was all a Democratic hoax. Rush Limbaugh insisted it was a trick of the ecoterrorists.

Yet I *knew* if there were really life out there, it had to look like us. We had been created in God's image, after all. How could there be different gods for different planets?

Of course, Mormons did believe in lots of gods, but all of the same species. They were all human gods, people like us who'd been tested in mortal life, passed their test, and moved up to godhood. But those gods worked in different universes. Our God was ruler over a multitude of worlds, so all his sentient species had to be human. The presence of these men and women from Tau Ceti simply proved what I'd known all along.

And yet, I couldn't help but ask.

"Zigmo," I said carefully, "if this isn't too personal, perhaps I could ask you something?"

Zigmo looked at me, his green eyes dull, his mouth slack. "Yes?"

"Do your people believe in God?"

Zigmo put his hand to his temple and shook his head. "Already," he muttered. "We're here one day, and already we get the question."

I felt a tingle of excitement. "So you mean there is religion on *all* worlds? *Everyone* believes in God?"

Zigmo lifted his hand almost dismissively. "Oh, there are thousands of different belief systems. The problem..." He paused. "...is that on each world there is *one* belief system that is the same on every other world. You can't know the grief this has caused."

I frowned. "I don't understand."

Zigmo glanced around the room. "Look, I don't want to talk here. Can we go somewhere?"

I looked around, too. "My office?"

Zigmo sighed. "I was thinking more of someplace far away. Is there a park anywhere nearby?"

One might have expected there to be tons of security keeping an eye on every move the aliens made, but they weren't prisoners, after all, and since they looked just like us, and had monitored us a few days in advance to be able to replicate our clothing, getting out of the building was no problem.

I directed our steps northward and westward, studying Zigmo's reactions to New York life. He seemed neither impressed nor fascinated. I was an Earthling, and I still found the place incredible. It was a bit deflating to realize there was not even any anthropological interest on Zigmo's part. He mostly looked at the sidewalk as we walked. When we passed Central Synagogue, he sighed.

But when we finally entered Central Park, he stopped and took a deep breath. "Those animals," he said, pointing to a horse drawing a buggy, "are beautiful. And those plants— just lovely. That's the best part of traveling."

He saw the look on my face and shook his head. "Of course there is evolution, so life takes a different path on every world. But *people*, you know we are all the same everywhere."

"How is that possible? If it's just evolution?"

"Your god and my god and everyone else's god want people to look like them, so he guides that one evolutionary pathway."

I had never thought about it. While it made sense on one level, the news also left me feeling a little uneasy. It was almost like receiving a revelation, and yet it was a decidedly unspiritual experience.

"Do you believe in Jesus?" I asked.

"Who's Jesus?"

"The Savior. The Messiah. The Son of God."

Zigmo breathed heavily. "No. We believe in Krean. The Savior. The Messiah. The Son of God."

I stopped. "Was he crucified?"

"Crucified?"

"Nailed to a cross."

"You people. No. Krean was beheaded. And Sissinu was drowned. And Kgrlbrk was burned."

"Who are Sissinu and K-kgr-whatever?"

"The messiahs of some of the other planets we've visited. *Everyone* has a messiah."

My mind was whirling. Every planet had their own messiah? Bruce R. McConkie in *Mormon Doctrine* had said that Jesus had come to our planet because ours was simultaneously the most righteous and most wicked, but that he was the savior of the entire universe. Just as the Nephites had to worship a Redeemer who lived on the far side of the world, people on other planets had to worship a Redeemer from across the night sky.

"Everyone?" I repeated.

"Every world we've visited so far," said Zigmo sadly. "Every single one. And each messiah was raised from the dead to lead his followers."

A young woman with a poodle on a leash walked by, and Zigmo's eyes lit up briefly. Then he looked at me and sighed again.

"Why does this make you sad?" I asked. "Doesn't it prove that your own belief system is true?"

Zigmo laughed. We'd come upon a bench by this time and sat down. "Don't you see the implications?"

"Why, yes. God is real."

Zigmo shook his head. "Perhaps. We wondered at first if some previous civilization had just seeded the various planets with humans and left us all a similar religious story to follow, but really, there'd be *some* divergence in appearance, and there is virtually none. And telling us about a messiah before the fact just isn't what we find in the historical record."

"So it *is* true," I said, smiling.

A Latina pushing a stroller with two babies walked by. Another woman stooped over to look at the infants and gushed with baby talk. Zigmo watched in apathy.

"Who is this Jesus to your God?" asked Zigmo carefully. "You said 'the son'?"

"Well, yes, he's God's firstborn son," I said and then stopped.

"You're starting to get the point."

I watched as a squirrel darted across the path in front of us. Zigmo smiled at its fluffy tail. "So God had two dozen firstborn sons?" I said slowly.

"So far. But I expect that with one hundred billion stars in this galaxy alone, there must be close to five hundred million inhabited planets yet to be discovered. Perhaps a billion. Even more."

I snapped my fingers. "But God has more than one wife! He could have a firstborn son with each of them!"

"God has five hundred million wives? A billion?" asked Zigmo sadly. "Is that really the kind of future we see for ourselves?"

An eternity of sex. It sounded appealing to me. "Well, we know there is polygamy in heaven…"

"You think there is only one righteous man for every five hundred million righteous women?"

I frowned. "Maybe 'firstborn' is just a metaphor of some kind. Maybe it just means 'beloved' or 'dedicated.'"

"Think about it a bit more. Wasn't your Jesus supposedly perfect from the beginning?"

"Yes?"

"So if God has five hundred million, or a billion—we don't know how many planets he has—perfect children, what does he want with *us*?"

"Why, he loves *all* of us."

Zigmo didn't say anything for a long moment. A butterfly floated by, but even this didn't elicit a smile. "So even though there are five hundred million righteous women for every one righteous man, God had five hundred million perfect sons and not a single perfect daughter to be a messiah?"

I felt decidedly uncomfortable again. Why was Zigmo saying all these things? I'd just discovered the gospel was undeniably true, and he was making me unhappy about it. I wanted to hit him.

Suddenly, I had a new thought. "What about Kolob?" I said. "Do you know Kolob?"

Zigmo nodded wearily. "That name is the same on every planet. So we know God lives there. But we haven't yet found it. Of course, we've only visited a handful of planets so far."

"But you *could* actually fly to Kolob?" I asked, wonderingly. "You could get to heaven without dying first?"

"That makes you happy?"

I stared at my hands. "No," I said. "No, it doesn't."

"I didn't think so."

I began to wonder if this Kartak Drive which had enabled the people of Tau Ceti to travel between star systems was something that God hadn't wanted anyone to develop. We still had free agency, of course, so perhaps he couldn't prevent it. Was traveling between stars and searching for Kolob like building the Tower of Babel?

"Sheesh, Zigmo, are there other things I'm missing?"

Zigmo laughed. "You won't fully understand the ramifications for months yet. I probably should let you remain blissfully unaware. You'll find that this knowledge won't help you feel closer to God or inspire you to be more righteous. In fact, it'll do just the opposite. We're debating stopping our explorations altogether. There were benefits to believing we were the center of God's universe."

Galileo all over again.

"No," I said. "I want to know."

Zigmo leaned over and pinched my arm, hard.

"Ow!" I said. "What'd you do that for?"

"Was that a sin?" asked Zigmo with a smile.

I frowned again.

"Who forgives me for that? Krean or Jesus? Is the messiah of each world the messiah only of the inhabitants of that world? Is Krean my redeemer even if I am light years from his planet? If his reach is so far, why isn't he the messiah of this world already? Who gets jurisdiction?"

I stared in confusion.

"And what happens when people start migrating? If someone from Tau Ceti moves to a planet around Epsilon Indi, do they have to change messiahs? Who is the messiah of interstellar space? If you're an ambassador and travel regularly between two worlds, do you need two messiahs?"

"Stop, Zigmo, you're confusing me."

Maybe he was simply lying. Perhaps he'd done research on our belief systems and he'd done on our clothing and knew what to say to confuse us. This could all be a plot of some sort.

He laughed bitterly. "You think you've just discovered 'the answer,' but I assure you, it raises more questions than you've ever had before."

"Maybe…maybe we shouldn't tell anybody else."

"You think we've brought you scientific advancements and peace. You don't know the religious and political upheaval in your future."

I clenched my jaw. "Well, the others in your group haven't said anything yet. Why'd *you* have to open your mouth?"

"They aren't believers."

I stared at him. "How can they not believe? With all this evidence?"

"Don't you have people on your planet who refuse to believe the most obvious and well-proven of things?"

I thought of those who still didn't believe in climate change. I thought of the fringe of society, still numerous, who believed our president was a Muslim and not even an American. Another idea began to form in my mind.

"I want to show you more of the park," I said. "It's the biggest urban park on the planet."

"It's quite lovely. The worst part of being on the ship is being away from nature."

We walked a long time in silence. I was trying to decide what to do. If I had been a Catholic or Baptist or Jew or Buddhist, would Zigmo's words have affected me so? Would he tell a different story to each diplomat, for some ulterior purpose I couldn't know?

But if what he said *was* true, how could I prevent the whole Earth from hearing about it?

How was it that confirmation brought doubt?

What was I going to do?

"We're still in the city?" Zigmo asked finally.

"This area is called the Ramble," I explained. "I like it because it's so remote, even in the midst of millions of people." We stopped to catch our breath. Now I'd find out if this alien being could really read my mind.

"It's beautiful," Zigmo said sadly. "Remote in the midst of millions."

I put my hand on his shoulder, and he turned to look at me. Then I put my other hand on his opposite shoulder and looked at him.

It had to be done.

He smiled weakly.

I put my hands around Zigmo's throat and began to squeeze. He looked mildly surprised but did not put up a fight. Only at the end, when instinct finally kicked in, did he begin to struggle, but by then it was too late.

I stood over Zigmo's lifeless body a moment later and wondered if I needed forgiveness from Krean as well as from Jesus. If the victim were not an Earthling, was I guiltless before *my* messiah?

Now I began to wonder if Zigmo were part of another religion altogether, and was sent as a human sacrifice, to ignite an interstellar war so his people could take over the Earth.

Human sacrifice. God gave his billion only begotten sons to be sacrificed for the hundreds of trillions of others teeming on every habitable planet for thousands of light years. Yet perhaps *one* person from Tau Ceti had to be sacrificed on Earth to be the liaison messiah between our two worlds.

I giggled.

Then I held myself tightly. I started to pray, but I immediately began wondering if I was simply being monitored on a large computer system on Kolob. Was God nothing more than another alien? At death, would my spirit be caught up in a tractor beam back to that planet? Was Zigmo there now? Where would there be room for all the zillions of spirits that had ever lived? Would we need interstellar travel to get from one heaven to another?

Was Outer Darkness the void between star systems? And was it so large because that's where most spirits ended up?

I started running through the Ramble, as fast as I could go. I ran until my chest hurt and kept running. As I ran, my mind became clearer. I would go to Salt Lake and talk face to face with the prophet. He'd be able to solve everything.

The prophet. And there had to be one on every planet. A billion prophets in our galaxy alone. And that was assuming our god wasn't also the god over the hundred billion other galaxies in the known universe.

God couldn't possibly be so great he could talk to so many people, and that was even if he spoke to one single person per planet. He could never pay attention to the prayers of four or five billion more on each of those billion planets. The numbers were…they were astronomical.

I stopped by a tree and leaned over, holding my side, laughing again. I could feel my sanity slipping away. All this information was sending my brain into overload. We'd always wondered what monumental revelations an alien race might bring us and how we might react. For decades, we heard rumors we'd already made contact but that government authorities were keeping the news secret because "the people" wouldn't be able to handle it. It never occurred to me that hearing the story we already knew would be the news which would send us over the edge.

Walking slowly back south toward the UN, I looked at my watch. I'd surely missed further talks and discussions by the alien delegation. Zigmo's absence would obviously be noticed by now. I'd have to play it cool but still dissuade the others from establishing full diplomatic relations with the Tau Ceti team.

I saw some pigeons on the sidewalk and scowled. Then I caught a bus heading down. I got off a couple of blocks from the UN and brushed myself off, making sure I looked presentable. As I approached the entrance, my mouth fell open.

Zigmo was standing there waiting.

Was he just playing mind games all this time? Was everything we'd talked about simply a fantasy he'd made take place in my brain? Maybe it was a test of some sort.

But had I failed that test? Or passed it?

Perhaps Zigmo had been resurrected, even though it had not been three days. Then again, he'd never said that every messiah took three days to rise from the dead.

"Come on," he said, offering his hand. I reached out hesitantly toward him. "We have much more to discuss. Let's go in and join the others."

He smiled, and we walked into the building together.

Half Marathon Man

Sandor hated going to the dentist. His mother had hated the ordeal, too, and so hadn't brought Sandor to the dentist till he was fully twelve years old. Strange, really, considering she didn't seem to mind inflicting pain herself, always seeming to enjoy spanking him with a belt any time he ever did anything wrong.

By the time Sandor finally did go to the dentist, he had a mouthful of cavities, and having them filled two at a time still took several visits. Lying trapped in the chair with a huge needle coming right toward his face was the stuff of nightmares. When Sandor had read William Goldman's *Marathon Man* in college, the torture scene where the Nazi drills into the nerves of the prisoner's teeth made him forsake dentists altogether. It had been two years since his last cleaning and check-up.

Sandor stood in front of the door. Ofelia Corazon. A woman couldn't be too mean, he thought. But then, she was Asian. He'd seen movies with evil female Asian villains.

Of course, some evil female Asian villains were hot.

Stop it.

He opened the door and walked to the receptionist. A black woman. He wasn't sure if that was good or bad. Was the place even accredited? "Sandor Martin here for a cleaning," he said cheerily, hoping he didn't sound nervous.

"Hello, Mr. Martin," the woman said with a friendly smile. Her teeth were very white. "Is this your first time with us?" Even though the woman was sitting, Sandor could tell she had a big butt. He couldn't help but wonder what it would be like for her to straddle him.

Sandor quietly pinched his hand. Heavenly Father was going to punish him for having such wicked thoughts. *Why* had he thought such things right before seeing the dentist? He was doomed.

"Yes, my boss recommended you," Sandor replied. "I work for Backpacker. My dental insurance is Oregon Dental."

The receptionist took down all the appropriate information, and then Sandor went to sit in a black leather chair near a water cooler and a coffee maker in the lobby. Coffee, he thought, shaking his head. Not only a sin for Mormons, but surely a sin for teeth in general. And how could the hygienists stand working on patients with coffee breath? The mere thought almost made Sandor ill.

He did like the black leather, though.

Sandor looked at the magazines on the coffee table, hoping to calm his nerves. *Time, Mother Jones, Good Housekeeping, Gamers, The Advocate, National Geographic...* Wait a minute. *The Advocate*? That looked like a gay magazine. Sandor glanced about the room. There was a poster advertising a protest march for fast-food workers beside the water cooler. Another flyer behind the coffee maker announced a meeting in support of the postal service.

Sandor wondered if Filipinos were usually so political. He'd come close to picking up a Thai porn video the one time he'd gone into one of those stores. But he'd been strong and left with nothing but his dignity.

Another flyer announcing a march in support of immigrants was posted on a different wall, and a rainbow flag hung in the corner. Sandor suppressed a wave of nausea. A rainbow flag? How could people be so decadent? Weren't dental offices supposed to have cheap paintings of scenic vistas? They were probably breaking a Dental Association rule with this stuff.

Sandor felt a drop of sweat forming on his forehead. He was in a den of iniquity. He should just get up and leave.

"Sandor?" said a young woman with blue hair who'd appeared in front of the receptionist's desk. At least she was white. And she was smiling. What choice did Sandor have? He stood up and followed the woman down a hall to a small room with a dentist's chair in the middle. "Have a seat," the woman said, smiling. "Is this your first time with us?"

"Yes." Sandor looked at the eyebrow piercing over the woman's left eye. A tattoo was just barely visible above where her scrub top ended. She was probably a slut.

Sandor was sure she was perfectly nice, of course. Just a slut. Part of him wondered what it would be like to date a slut.

He was going to marry a virgin in the temple.

He had a brief image of a head of blue hair bobbing back and forth in front of his waist.

He was going to hell. He knew it. And Heavenly Father was going to punish him here right now. He should leave.

Sandor sat down in the chair. His underarms felt damp. Things were sure different here in Portland than they'd been in Provo. He'd loved BYU, first as an undergraduate and then while attending the business school for his MBA. A first-class school at a first-class university. It was only religious prejudice that prevented them from becoming a PAC12 school. It was so easy to be good when surrounded by good people.

He wished he could have found a job in Salt Lake, but the best offer had come from Backpacker. He'd only been there a few weeks, but so far, he could tell a lot of his colleagues were Democrats. It was hard keeping his mouth shut, but he didn't want to get fired while still on probation. He wondered if a good paycheck was worth risking his soul by being around sinners all the time.

"I'm Nan," said the blue-haired young woman, reaching around Sandor's neck to affix a blue paper napkin. "Just sit back and relax." She handed him a pair of sunglasses.

Sandor leaned back in the chair, looking ahead at a photo on the wall of a woman chained to a huge tree. His stomach felt tense. "How long have you been working here?" Sandor asked, to make conversation. The chains kept drawing his attention.

"About three months. I really like it. Dr. Corazon is great."

Three months? Sandor's right foot started twitching. The girl didn't even know what she was doing. She was going to butcher him.

Well, he deserved it, with all his sinful thoughts. Why had Heavenly Father plagued him with such a high testosterone level? Sexual sin was about as bad as it got. Why couldn't he have the urge to commit lesser sins, like stealing or lying?

Perhaps true greatness ran both ways. He could either be a great, huge sinner or a great, righteous man on his way to godhood. Mediocrity wasn't in his future either way. That's what being chosen to come to Earth in the latter days meant.

"Have you noticed any trouble with your teeth?" asked Nan, sitting down next to him.

"No," Sandor lied. He had extreme sensitivity when drinking cold drinks. "Dear Heavenly Father," he prayed silently, "help me through this. I'll be good if you help me through this."

"Since this is your first visit, we're going to start with some X-rays." Nan shoved a huge piece of cardboard into his mouth, twisting it this way and that. It was uncomfortable but bearable. Nan laid a heavy blanket that must have had lead in it over his chest, walked out of the room, clicked a button, and came back in. Then she shoved another piece of cardboard into his mouth and repeated the procedure. Before long she was finished. "I'll send these off to be developed, so they'll be ready for Dr. Corazon after I do your cleaning."

Sandor rubbed his cheek. He was sure to get a sore from all the rough treatment. Of course, he sometimes fantasized about a woman slapping him while they were having sex. Or pinching his nipples hard. Or a woman biting his neck hard enough to leave a mark. But rough treatment for roughness' sake wasn't all that satisfying. Sandor wondered if the girl could see his "eternal smile" through his work shirt. If she could tell he was wearing garments, she might be making this rougher than it had to be. Of course, he had no real proof, but he still wondered.

"Have you lived in Portland long?" Nan asked after removing the lead vest and sitting back in her chair.

"Just a few weeks. How did you know I wasn't a native?"

"Lots of people move here all the time. It's a great city. Are you liking it so far?"

"So far." There was a Single Adult dance at the stake center this Saturday night, which would be a nice gift after his long run. He ran at least six miles every day, but on weekends, he ran further. He felt righteous punishing his body. It made him a better man. Sandor was looking forward to the dance. He wondered if there were any pure Mormon girls outside of Utah. He wanted a pure Mormon girl.

"Now relax." Nan lowered his seat. "I'm going to use an ultrasonic vibrator on your teeth. It'll break up the plaque and tartar very quickly. And it doesn't hurt a bit."

She hooked a plastic tube over Sandor's lower lip to suck up water.

Sandor had just a fleeting thought, wondering how a slightly larger sucking tube like that would feel on his penis.

God, why was he doing this? Why couldn't he keep his thoughts clean for even five minutes? He was a returned missionary. He was an elder in the Melchizedek priesthood. He was a virgin.

He was going to marry in the temple and become a god one day.

If masturbators were allowed in the temple. Why, *why* couldn't he control his sexual feelings? Heavenly Father expected it. Heavenly Father *demanded* it.

He remembered all those humiliating worthiness interviews with the bishop, every six months since he was twelve. And from the very start, he'd had to confess masturbating. Oh, he'd try and try not to masturbate, sometimes going one or even two weeks without, but eventually, he'd find himself fantasizing and fantasizing, growing more and more wicked, and wasting so much time that it was just better to whack off and be done with it.

Confessing was so mortifying, though, and he'd simply lied later while on his mission, afraid of being sent home. He'd kept up the lies with his leaders since returning, but that only made him feel more decadent. He was a grown man now, old enough to put these juvenile acts behind him. Why, *why* couldn't he be normal?

Nan inserted a tool into his mouth and turned on a machine that began whirring. Sandor felt the tool moving along his gum lines. As Nan had said, it didn't hurt, but it seemed to be squirting a lot of water into his mouth. He could feel the spray and hear the plastic tube gurgling away. As Nan worked, she continued talking. "I'm from San Francisco.

Finished my hygienist training a few months ago and decided to move up here and make a new start. My little boy loves his preschool. You okay? Your foot's wiggling."

Nan took the tool out of Sandor's mouth, and he forced his foot to remain still. "I'm fine," he said bravely. "So how long have you been married? You have other children?" Maybe she wasn't so bad after all. Maybe there were in fact some good people outside of Zion.

Nan laughed and thrust the tool back into Sandor's mouth. "Oh, no husband for me," she said. "Unh-unh. I had a gay friend donate sperm. I wanted to go to a clinic, but he wanted to try sex with a woman, so we did it his way." She laughed again. "His partner even watched."

Sandor was horrified to hear Nan speak like this but was even more horrified to realize his groin had twitched in response. This low-class woman was going to make him fantasize about even more evil acts. She was putting sinful ideas in his head. *That's* why good Mormons hardly ever associated with non-Mormons.

Heavenly Father, how much longer was this going to take? Sandor wanted to get out of there and get back to the office where he could focus his mind on work. Nan continued to talk, but Sandor forced himself to pray and blocked out the next few minutes. And then Nan turned off the ultrasonic machine. It was over. He could leave now.

It was so hard living "in" the world while not being part "of" the world. Every day was a battle, especially out here away from the center of Zion. What if he wasn't man enough to handle it?

"You had a lot of build-up," Nan said. "Do you brush regularly?"

"Of course." How rude.

"Do you floss?"

Sandor hesitated. "Not as much as I should." Meaning never.

"Do you have certain teeth you'd like to keep?" she asked. He was sure she was smiling, but he couldn't see her mouth through her paper mask.

"What's that supposed to mean?"

"Well, you should floss just the teeth you plan to keep."

"I plan to keep all of them!" Sandor snapped, irritated.

"Good. We like to hear that. Now I have to tell you, you're only going to keep the ones you floss, so you take it from there."

What a jerk, thought Sandor. Trying to humiliate him like that. Non-members knew nothing about how to encourage people through the Spirit. Every day that he had to mix with Gentiles, Sandor was more and more appreciative of the Gospel. He wondered if he should ask Nan the Golden Questions now that they were through. She might still make a good person, if she were Mormon.

He imagined sinning with her one last time before her baptism, but then *he'd* be sinning, too. That wouldn't work.

"Do you go to church?" he asked bluntly.

Nan looked at him in surprise. "That's kind of a personal question, isn't it?"

Personal? The woman was just describing sex with a voyeur looking on. "Do you believe in God?" Sandor pressed.

"Hmm," Nan said slowly. "Well, I believe in a Goddess."

Oh, brother, thought Sandor. But he might as well go through with it at this point. "What do you know about the Mormon Church?"

"The Prop 8 people?" She shrugged. "I know they're small-minded."

Sandor was stymied now. He'd been taught that no matter what the answer was to the original question, a good member always followed up by asking the second question, "Do you want to know more?" But that felt awkward now.

"Okay," said Nan, "we got most of the plaque and tartar off your teeth, but the ultrasonic vibrations don't get everything. We have to get the last of it with our scaler."

"Scaler?"

She held up a small tool with an ugly looking, curved point at the end. "Our pick."

Sandor felt something cold in his stomach. He took a deep breath as Nan reached in his mouth with the frightening pick and a small mirror on the end of another metal stick. She scraped at Sandor's teeth near his gum line, and every few seconds, it felt as if she was deliberately poking his gums and tearing them. She withdrew for a moment and brought back the plastic tube that sucked up water, spraying water into his mouth. "Lots of blood," explained Nan. "Your gums are very inflamed. You have the beginning stages of gum disease, and unless you start flossing, you really are going to lose all your teeth."

Lots of blood, thought Sandor, because you're cutting my gums on purpose. She was evil. She was a tool of the devil.

Or maybe she was Heavenly Father's way of punishing him for his stray thoughts.

She started scratching away again with the pick, and Sandor prayed some more. "Heavenly Father, you know I'm a brave man. I donate blood. I run half marathons. I do my Home Teaching. I obey the Word of Wisdom. I talk to people on the bus about the Book of Mormon. I fast twice a month instead of just the one time. You know I go above and beyond the call of duty. So I need you to bless me now. Please keep this woman from hurting me." After he said amen, he had one last thought. What would it be like to kiss this woman, his mouth full of blood?

Stop it. Stop it!

Sandor lay in the chair, staring up at a bright light on a mechanical arm. The sunglasses kept the light from hurting his eyes, but he could still feel Nan poking and tearing at his gums. How much more of this would he have to take? How much more of this did he *deserve*? He thought about work. Backpacker was a good company, with a good 401k and profit sharing.

His boss gave everyone three days off a year just to do volunteer work. Sandor had signed up for the two remaining days of this year he'd be eligible to help. He'd picked cleaning the Ronald McDonald House and picking up trash in the park. Nothing meaningful. Sandor liked working as a stake missionary and going on splits with the elders. It reminded him of his days as a missionary, the happiest time of his life, despite the masturbating.

Once, the four elders in his apartment had held a circle jerk, the first he'd had since his days as a Boy Scout. It had made him feel young and carefree again, though of course he'd never truly quite felt carefree, and doing it with other messengers of God had somehow made it feel less sinful. They'd only done it the one time, and no one ever talked about it again, but Sandor thought about that lovely day often. Somehow, that wonderful even if sinful release had led him to be an even better missionary.

He'd been bold and brave in Hungary, facing untold masses of people ignorant of the Gospel. He'd felt strong, knowing he had the Truth while they knew nothing about God, at least nothing accurate. It was great being on God's side, knowing you were right. He'd felt that feeling so strongly while being one of only a handful of Saints in Hungary, and he felt it while one of a multitude in Provo.

Why didn't he feel that here in Portland? Here he felt all alone against the world. Satan was so powerful in the Northwest. Sandor wasn't sure he was strong enough to resist. He was already thinking of rewarding himself for surviving the dentist by going back to the video store.

A piercing pain shot through Sandor's body. Nan was poking that infernal hook right on a raw nerve. She was a Nazi.

"Is that sensitive?" she asked.

"Uh-huh." He felt his groin twitch again.

"Looks like you might have a cavity. We'll have Dr. Corazon take a look in a bit."

The scraping and poking continued for a few more very long minutes, and then Nan seemed to be finished. Sandor sighed in relief.

"Now we'll floss, and then we'll polish your teeth."

She unrolled a long white thread from a little plastic box, wrapping the ends around different fingers, and then thrust her gloved fingers into Sandor's mouth. She squeezed the string between Sandor's back teeth, twisted and rubbed for a moment, sawing deep into his gums, and extracted the string. Then she went to the space between the next pair of teeth and continued, going first through Sandor's upper teeth and then through the lower ones. It felt as if she was cutting him every single time. He tasted iron.

He imagined her sitting on top of him, tying his hands to the bedposts with thick string.

"Lots of blood," Nan repeated. "You really need to start flossing daily." She squirted water into his mouth and sucked it up again with the plastic tube. The cold water hurt.

Sandor's groin twitched again. He could feel his erection struggling against his pants. He hoped Nan couldn't see it.

He hoped she could.

"Please, Heavenly Father," Sandor prayed.

"Your foot is wiggling again."

He forced his foot to remain still.

Nan took out another device, put some toothpaste on the end of it, and stuck it in Sandor's mouth. It had a minty taste, but it also felt like there was sand in it. Sandor almost gagged. Was she grinding down his teeth? Was this ordeal never going to end?

What would an eternal future of damnation and punishment feel like?

Every few moments, Nan withdrew, then sprayed water and sucked it out, and then continued polishing. Then finally, finally, she seemed to be finished.

"I'll go get your X-rays, and Dr. Corazon will be in in a moment."

Sandor tried to relax, but all he could see was the tree hugger on the wall. And the chains. A few minutes later, a short, petite Filipino woman came in and sat next to him. "Your teeth feel clean now?" she asked.

"Sure."

Nan mentioned some numbers Sandor didn't understand, and Dr. Corazon looked at two specific teeth. "You have a cavity we'll need to take care of. This other problem area is something we'll keep an eye on. You'll need to take good care of your teeth, or you'll have another cavity before long."

"Okay."

"You can make an appointment at the desk. We'll see you in a couple of weeks."

Wonderful, thought Sandor. He had to come back. He just abhorred dentists. Sometimes, he thought they created cavities on purpose to generate repeat business.

He wished Nan would be the one to give him his injection the next time he came.

The dentist left, and Nan began rummaging around in a cabinet. "You want a blue toothbrush, a purple one, or a green one?"

"Green," Sandor mumbled.

"I like green, too," said Nan. "I'm going to put some floss in here as well. And you should really use a mouthwash to help keep the germs down."

"Sure."

"You have any plans for the weekend?" She seemed to be making happy chatter now that she'd finished torturing him. He felt himself growing flaccid.

Here was his chance to mention church again. "Well, Saturday, I'm running a practice half marathon to get ready for next month's race, and then—"

"Really?" asked Nan. "You run?"

"Yes, and then Sunday—"

"I pegged you as someone who wasn't too careful with his body, considering your teeth."

Sandor didn't know what to say. She had tattoos and piercings, so who was she to talk?

Sandor wondered how it would feel to get a nipple piercing.

"I run, too," she said. "Want to run together Saturday morning?"

Sandor was completely nonplussed. Was she asking him on a *date*? A girl asking a guy? If the woman was the aggressor, wouldn't that make him less of a man? And why was a non-member asking out a Mormon? Was this Satan's way of pulling him even further away from the Gospel? Or the Lord's way of giving Sandor another chance to talk about the Church? He couldn't let himself be afraid of Nan, despite how brazen she was.

"Sure," he said slowly. "You ever get a runner's high?" He was going to tell her what it felt like to experience the Holy Ghost by making an analogy.

"No pain, no gain," she replied. "I always feel good after feeling bad first."

How strange, Sandor thought. He always felt bad after feeling good first. He looked at Nan's eyebrow piercing. He looked at her blue hair and the little part of her tattoo he could see above her scrubs. He looked at her breasts.

There was no sin in just running with the woman, was there? He knew he had a lot he could teach her. And just possibly, she had a few things she could teach him as well, even if it was through temptation. It was a test, and Heavenly Father gave his saints lots of tests in the last days. He was a good man, and he was going to pass those tests. He was going to marry a virgin in the temple and become a god one day.

Still, it might be nice just once *not* to talk about church. Pretend for just one day there was a life beyond it.

They arranged to meet at a park, and then Nan offered her hand. "It was a pleasure meeting you," she said.

"The pleasure was all mine." He wanted to hold onto her hand longer. He wished she would pinch him. Or scratch him.

"See you Saturday."

"Have a good day."

Sandor walked out of the examining room and down the hall to the receptionist's desk. He waited while the receptionist with the white teeth arranged his next visit. He looked about the waiting room at the poster for immigrants' rights. Then he walked out of the office in the direction of the bus stop. He ran the last few feet and caught the bus as it was pulling up. He held onto the handrail above him and headed downtown for work, staring at a young Hispanic woman's breasts the entire way.

The Blood Clot

I had a bladder the size of a walnut. Morgan always complained about it whenever we went on a trip. Or anytime we were out shopping together. Or when I woke him up from a sound sleep. Tonight was no different. "Jamala, I'm the man in his fifties," he said. "I'm the one who's supposed to be getting up in the middle of the night to pee, not you."

"I could always wear a diaper to bed if you prefer," I replied. "Or we could just put a plastic sheet on the mattress if that works better for you." He turned over and pretended to go back to sleep.

I kept the lights off so as not to disturb Morgan any further, and even though we hadn't changed the layout of our furniture in probably fifteen years, I walked right into the coffee table. "Ow! Damn! Mmph!" I put my hand over my mouth and tried to stifle my shouts. I sat on the coffee table and put my hand on my right shin. The pain was excruciating. I knew I'd done damage. I wondered if I'd fractured the bone.

After a moment, the pain lessened to something almost bearable, and I limped my way to the bathroom. We had an old Craftsman cottage, so obviously there was no en suite bathroom. In fact, there was only one in the entire house, though we had three bedrooms. One of the bedrooms had been turned into an office that both Morgan and I shared, and the other was Bradley's old room. He was across town at the University of Washington now and only visited briefly to do laundry once every couple of weeks. I was thinking of turning his room into a sewing room. I'd always wanted to quilt in my spare time. Maybe now was my chance.

In the bathroom, I turned on the light, shielding my eyes for a moment from the glare. Then I took a breath and looked down at my leg.

There was a dark swelling the size and shape of half a baseball. I'd always had a problem with platelets and wondered for a second if I was going to bleed to death. After I urinated, I walked slowly and carefully back out to the living room and sat down on the sofa, pulling a blanket Bradley had bought for us while on his mission to Thailand up over me. It was 38 degrees outside, so about 55 in the house. I wondered if I should get an ice pack from the freezer to apply to my shin, but I was too afraid to touch it with anything at all.

I could hear Morgan's light snoring through the wall and knew he wouldn't miss me, so I sat on the sofa another half hour. Then I took a deep breath and made my way back to the bathroom and looked at my leg again. The half baseball was gone now. Instead, there was a general swelling that covered half my shin. I breathed a sigh of relief. At least I wasn't going to die.

I shook my head. I was not the type of woman who thrived on drama, but I had to admit, I did always have the slightest tendency toward hypochondria. Still, looking down at my leg, an article I'd read on Yahoo recently popped into my head. A woman had stubbed her toe and bruised it badly, and a week later, a blood clot had dislodged from it and gone right to her lungs and killed her.

Was I going to die? I could have a clot break free at any moment and travel to my lungs, or my heart, or my brain.

I was only fifty-one. I wasn't ready to die.

Had Joseph Smith been ready? Had Abinadi? Was anyone ever truly ready?

I remembered a car commercial that had played repeatedly last month: a young man brings coffee to Santa, carries his bag up a long flight of stairs, mends Santa's clothes, all in the hopes of getting a car for Christmas, which Santa in fact gives him. I suddenly realized I was not the most pleasant woman in the world. If I was about to meet my Maker, maybe I'd better spend my last few days being nice to people.

I walked carefully back to the kitchen and looked at the clock on the microwave. It was 4:00. Too early to start breakfast. I limped to the office and rummaged around for a few minutes until I found some blank greeting cards featuring beautiful photographs of exotic flowers. I'd bought them on sale a couple of years ago but had never bothered sending them to anyone. I addressed one to my mother, one to my aunt, one to my sister, and one to my cousin Ellie, my favorite person in the world.

I hadn't spoken to her in months. Even for Christmas, all I'd said in my cards to friends and family was "Merry Christmas!" I sat down now and filled out the blank spaces on both leaves of each card. Then I affixed some Forever stamps featuring bluebirds to the envelopes and sealed them shut. I realized that blood clot could detach in just a few hours. I had to act as if today was my last day on Earth, because it might well be.

I went online and donated $30 to the University of Utah library, $30 to *Sunstone* magazine, $30 to *Dialogue*, and $50 to Signature Books. That was about the extent of my superfluous funds, but I added a $25 donation to Doctors without Borders. If it turned out I discovered the Church wasn't true once I died, I wanted to still have made at least one useful contribution at the end.

It was almost 6:00 now, so I made my way back to the kitchen and started frying some bacon. When I heard Morgan bumping around in the bedroom, I cracked four eggs and started scrambling them. He came out a few minutes later on his way to the bathroom and looked at me in astonishment. "What's up?" he said. I normally only cooked a real breakfast on weekends.

"Today's a special day," I replied.

He looked bewildered. "And why is that?"

I couldn't very well tell him I was about to die, so I smiled and said, "It's the first day of the rest of our lives." He gave me a funny look and continued on to the bathroom. I put two slices of bread in the toaster.

We had a quiet, muted breakfast, it still being too early to talk. Morgan volunteered to do the dishes while I got dressed for work. Then while he was getting dressed, I inspected the dishes in the drainboard. As I expected, there was egg still on one plate and one fork. It drove me absolutely crazy that my husband was incapable of washing a dish.

Normally, I'd have put the offending items back in the sink and asked Morgan to rewash them, but today I thought, "I don't want Morgan's last memory of me to be henpecking." So I rewashed the dishes myself.

Morgan took the car, as he had to travel to Kirkland, and I caught the bus, as I was only going to downtown Seattle. I'd wanted to quit work for such a long time, but somehow, realizing this could be my last day, things didn't frustrate me as they normally might. When the man one cubicle over started clipping his nails and I could see slivers of keratin flying through the air, I just shrugged and let it go. When he played his music too loudly, I put it out of my mind. No need to be a harpy on my last day.

In some respects, I was tempted to tell everyone exactly what I thought of them, but of course the problem was that I might *not* have a blood clot kill me. I had to act simultaneously as if today was my last day *and* as if it wasn't. It was Friday anyway, so it was relatively easy to let things pass.

On the way home, the bus was full. I stood next to a young man about thirty who had no intention of giving up his seat. I thought of saying something to make him feel guilty, but then I just shrugged and held on to the bar over my head. Maybe the weight on my leg would make the clot dislodge sooner. Maybe I'd finally get to see my father and grandparents again. And the baby I lost at birth all those years ago. I hoped Clara's body had housed a spirit at least briefly. I'd fantasized so many times about meeting her.

Perhaps finally, finally, this test was over and I could go home. I put a little extra weight on my right leg, hoping to loosen the clot, but then I shifted my weight back to the other. It wouldn't do to commit suicide when I was almost through anyway.

I arrived home just after 6:00, a full seventy minutes after Morgan returned home. I looked at the curb as I walked up to the house. No recycle bin. No garbage bin. No yard waste bin. It irritated the hell out of me. Morgan *never* put out the trash unless I nagged him. It drove me absolutely bananas. So many things about Morgan drove me crazy. Sometimes I wondered if I even wanted to spend eternity with him.

But I put my bag down on the porch and walked to the side of the house and wheeled the heavy recycling bin to the curb. Then I walked back and carried both the smaller bins. I picked up my bag again and went inside.

"Hi, honey," said Morgan, giving me a peck. "What's for dinner?"

"I had a great day, dear," I replied. "How was yours?"

"It was fine. I'm famished."

I bit my lip, irritated with myself for the sarcasm. Not the way I wanted to act on my last day. I turned the oven on, slid a pizza onto a tray, and went to change clothes. That bruise was really ugly, I thought, examining it again. Good. Maybe I'd die in my sleep tonight. I'd always wanted to die in bed when it was my time to go.

As we ate dinner, Morgan told me all about his day, the meetings he'd been in, the projects he was working on. Having been up since the middle of the night, I could barely keep my eyes open. I smiled and said, "Uh-huh," at regular intervals.

"I'll do the dishes, dear," Morgan said magnanimously after we finished eating. A pizza tray and two plates. Still, I smiled and thanked him.

When he was off in the bathroom brushing his teeth, I inspected the dishes. Cheese still on one plate and burned tomato paste on part of the pizza tray. I gritted my teeth and rewashed the dishes. I was not going to say anything.

But it wasn't enough simply to *act* nice. I had to feel it in my heart or I'd still miss out on the Celestial Kingdom. Morgan's a man, I told myself. He can't help being a slob any more than I can help having breasts. I didn't get to choose the size of my breasts, and he doesn't get to choose the size of his inability to help around the house. It's part of his DNA. Being mad about it is like being mad my breasts are too small. Morgan never makes an issue of my breasts. I'm not going to make an issue about his housework. It is what it is.

I soon calmed down and went to sit on the sofa. On Friday nights, Morgan and I watched Bill Moyers. After the show this evening, I pulled out the chess board and we played our regular Friday night game. Only tonight, I let Morgan win.

"Checkmate," he said finally. "Whoo hoo!"

I was way too tired for sex, but Morgan always liked to start the weekend off "with a bang," as he put it, so I gave him a blow job, and then I fell fast asleep.

I got up around 3:00 to pee. Morgan moaned in bed beside me as I climbed out. I walked more carefully tonight, not wanting to bang my leg again. Something like that would almost surely dislodge a clot. While I was prepared to go right away, I didn't totally mind staying around for a few more days. The daffodils were starting to pop up out of the ground. Spring was almost here.

Rather than go back to bed, I turned the radio in the living room on low and listened to soft classical music as I dozed on the sofa.

I had hardly finished rewashing the breakfast dishes when Bradley bounced into the house carrying his laundry basket. "Mom," he said, giving me a kiss, "I have so much to do today. Do you mind doing my laundry for me?" It was the same thing every time. He was always too busy. Rather than get angry, though, I looked at my son as if this were the last opportunity I'd see him for many, many years. I felt so overwhelmed I almost cried.

"No problem. You do what you have to do."

"You're the best, Mom." He kissed me and ran out of the house.

"You let that boy walk all over you," Morgan said, turning the TV on to Melissa Harris-Perry. I just laughed.

I wasn't sure how to spend the day, however. If this was my last day, should I read that new Patricia Cornwell novel? Or should I reread my favorite book of all time, *Little Women*? Should I just read the Book of Mormon? Or maybe the New Testament? If I *knew* with certainty this was my last day of life, which book would I choose?

The problem was that I didn't know. And I wanted to read Patricia Cornwell. So I picked up my eBook reader and began to read. The words felt like caffeine flowing through my veins after too long without. There was no other way to describe that glorious feeling.

It wasn't as if there wouldn't be a copy of the scriptures on the Other Side. I could always read from that tomorrow.

I rewashed the dishes after dinner, we watched a DVD of *The Last Voyage*, and then it was time for bed. Saturday night was always "real" sex night, which meant the missionary position. I liked this best because all I had to do was lie there and moan at appropriate moments while I planned my Sunday supper.

I had enjoyed sex at the beginning, but Morgan only had three positions, and it was hard staying interested after so many years. I hoped there really was something to this polyandry the Church had recently admitted. In any event, after I died in my sleep tonight, I'd be several years without sex of any kind, so maybe it would turn out to be interesting again the next time I saw Morgan.

I wondered if gods took sex vacations from each other every few years to keep sex exciting throughout eternity.

My leg hurt if I slept on my side, and I snored if I slept on my back, so after a couple of hours, I went back out to the sofa and turned on the classical music station again. It was Sunday now. It would be nice to die on the Sabbath. I touched my leg gingerly, afraid to dislodge a clot but too curious to resist. Boy, that still hurt.

It was going to be so great to see Heavenly Father and Jesus again. I hadn't seen them in over fifty years.

I rewashed the breakfast dishes while Morgan dressed for church, and then I hurried to dress as well. As we walked into the chapel, the bishop greeted us. "So nice you could make it the last Sunday of the month," he said. "I see you're keeping your New Year's resolution of doing the bare minimum to be considered officially active."

I wanted to say, "Believe me, Bishop, as boring as you make these meetings, I'm sure God gives me full credit for showing up even just once a month." But as I expected to die right there in the chapel, what I said instead was, "You don't even have to make a resolution to be charming, do you? It just comes out naturally."

I said it sweetly, but I wondered if that statement was any better than the one I'd censored. I figured I'd better repent when the sacrament was passed. I didn't have much time and certainly couldn't wait till next week, or till the end of February, as it would probably wind up.

The talks were boring, as usual, and I struggled to stay focused. This was going to be my last Sunday, I kept telling myself with a smile. As the day's meetings dragged on, though, I began hoping my clot would break free right there and then. Anything to spare me. I found myself touching my leg at intervals, then stopping as I realized what I was trying to do. Leaving Relief Society meeting, one of the sisters took my arm and said, "I just love the way you let your hair go natural. Not many women can carry off wrinkles and gray the way you do."

I looked back at her, gritting my teeth but smiling. Interacting with other people so often involved trying to patch the outflow of candor trying to escape from my soul at the slightest injury.

But was it right to spend my last days being namby-pamby? Was dying a doormat really the way to slide into heaven?

What kind of god wanted bootlicking from fellow gods?

I remembered that car commercial. I wanted to be on Santa's good side. So I smiled and said, "I don't believe in being artificial like some people." Then I bit my lip again. Damn, I was still being a bitch.

We picked up some fried chicken on the way home. I got out our special green ceramic Sunday plates and divvied out the food. Then I put a can of diet Coke by my plate and a can of diet Sprite by Morgan's. Morgan and I talked about what life might be like in the Millennium, and what terrible trials might be in store for us during the Last Days.

Today was my Last Day, I thought, and I couldn't even face the mediocre trials I'd faced over the last few hours. What kind of Latter-day Saint was I? And I still didn't know if I'd done the right thing by softening my responses at church, or if that was worse than being candid. I didn't know if it was right to attend meetings my last day, or if I'd just wasted three precious hours. Even knowing this might be my last day, I still didn't know how to live.

Should I send happy, peppy emails to my friends this afternoon, or should I call Ellie and share all the doubts I had about Morgan and Bradley and work and the Church and everything else?

What was the right way to live?

I rewashed the dishes after Morgan finished, but then I noticed he'd left his empty soda can four inches from the recycle bin.

I walked out to the living room, where Morgan was flipping through the PBS guide. "Honey?" I said.

"Yes?" He looked up at me with a contented expression, probably already looking forward to my special Sunday dinner. I planned Italian sausage with potato soup, my favorite.

"Put your goddamn can in the goddamn recycle bin."

His mouth fell open.

I smiled and walked to the office and picked up the phone. I dialed Ellie, rubbing my leg calmly as I waited for her to answer.

Poison Ivy Testimonies

I had just turned twelve and was finally eligible to participate in Girls Camp. Our stake in Asheville had arranged for us all to spend a week in the Pisgah National Forest. My parents were a little worried because a woman had been raped there a couple of months ago, and a gang of teenagers had tied an old couple to a tree a month before that. But our youth leaders promised that the Holy Ghost would be with us and watch over us, so my parents reluctantly agreed I could take part.

"Hannah," I said into my cell phone, "I'm going!" Hannah had been my best friend since we were Sunbeams.

"That's great, Diana!" she replied. "Julie and Connie will be there, too!" We were all Beehives in our ward. Julie and Connie were a little on the dim side, but nice enough. My mother always chided me if I said anything like that about them at dinner, and I guessed I was in fact a little snooty at times, a weakness I tried steadily to overcome. My teachers at church often tried to single me out by giving me extra opportunities to grow. Julie and Connie sometimes snickered about it.

But Hannah, Hannah I liked completely. She was sweet, with dimples, the friendliest smile, wavy auburn hair, and always had a kind word for others. Her testimony never wavered, while mine did. She was the type to grow up to be

Relief Society president one day. I was the type to become someone's service project.

"We'll get to hike and swim and tell stories around the campfire," I continued.

"But we'll have to sleep in tents," Hannah countered. "They won't spring for the cabins. And we probably won't get to shower for a week."

"No parents, though," I pointed out. "That has to count for something."

"But my sister Victoria will be there," said Hannah. "And she'll report anything I do back to my mom."

"Well, *I* haven't got a sister," I said. I had a younger brother who was ten and would be glad to see me go. I couldn't say I'd miss Calvin much, either. "And you know I'll keep you out of trouble."

"You always see the positive." Hannah laughed. "What would I do without you?"

Normally during the summer, Hannah and I rode our bikes through the neighborhood, sneaked to the store to buy lipstick which we wiped off before our parents could see, and talked about what life would be like four long years from now when we would finally be allowed to date. I didn't particularly like boys, and didn't really mind not going out with them the way the other girls at school did, the way the other girls at church kept wishing they could.

Just spending time with Hannah was enough. We slept at each other's house, stayed up late watching 1930's horror movies on DVD, and talked about what we'd do when we grew up. Hannah wanted to marry a returned missionary and have five kids. I wanted to go on a mission myself, maybe to Africa or Nova Scotia, and become an epidemiologist.

"Too bad you're not a boy," Hannah said once. "You'd make the perfect husband."

I took it as a compliment.

I wondered if anyone would be bitten by a bug out in the woods during Girls Camp and catch a new disease. Part of me thought about how my parents would be upset by such a thing, and part of me was fascinated by the possibility.

The big day was only a week away, and on a bright Monday morning, all the girls met at the stake center. We squeezed into six minivans driven by Young Women's leaders, and we headed for camp an hour away. The first thing we did was set up our tents, which took quite a while, as not even the adults seemed to know what to do.

Brother Campbell, the first counselor in the stake presidency, was setting up his tent by himself. He was the lone male present, here to ensure our safety, in case the Holy Ghost alone wasn't enough. I finished our tent first and then went with Hannah to help some others, where I heard Sister Bradford talking to Sister Goodson. "I better get a shiny gold doorknob on my mansion in heaven."

Sister Goodson replied with a smile, "I'm happy with just brass."

"Sounds like a Telestial attitude to me," Sister Bradford returned.

"Lusting after gold isn't a Celestial one," Sister Goodson said, smiling back.

This was going to be a great week, I thought, nudging Hannah to listen to the conversation. My parents had talked to me about the perverse satisfaction I felt in discovering that people at church weren't perfect. "The Church isn't for the spiritually healthy," my dad said. "It's for the spiritually ill."

"Then I should be right at home," I replied. "What are you complaining for?"

My parents just looked at each other, not knowing what to say. I felt sorry for them, having such a difficult daughter.

Of course, Calvin was no prize, either.

Being at camp with Hannah was fun. It was a time to forget about parents and the upcoming school year and Gentile friends and television and cell phones. But the realities of the place soon began to take their toll. It was hot. There was no air conditioning. There were bugs. Everyone was covered in mosquito bites by the morning of the second day. I wondered if I had caught some new disease myself. Six of the girls had poison ivy rashes by the end of the third day.

The food was terrible, and there wasn't enough of it after hours and hours of hiking every day. We did spend an hour every afternoon playing a Mormon trivia game or singing hymns or doing some role-playing exercises about how to tell our non-member friends about the Church. The worst part, though, was that at night around the campfire, instead of telling ghost stories or doing other fun things, we had to listen to stories about the pioneers crossing the plains. We were in

North Carolina, for goodness' sake. What did we need to hear about that stuff for?

Hannah, Julie, Connie, and I made up for it by sharing a tent and staying up past lights out and telling our own stories. "Did you hear the one about the couple that drove to a secluded spot to neck?" Hannah asked.

"Mormons don't neck," said Julie.

"Well, these weren't Mormons. Or at least, the boy wasn't. The girl was, and she said she didn't want to go to any secluded spot. She said she'd heard there was a crazy serial killer out there with a hook for a hand."

"Ooh." Did I mention that Julie was dim-witted?

"But the boy took her out there anyway and tried to start kissing her. She kept pushing him away and he kept trying to fondle her."

"That's just like a non-Mormon boy," said Connie, nodding. She was only six months older than I was and couldn't even go to youth dances yet. With all our parents monitoring what television shows and movies we could see, I wondered why she thought she knew anything about this. I at least read books. A library card was a useful thing.

"When the boy kept trying to feel her up," Hannah continued, "she started bearing her testimony. The boy finally got so mad he threw the car into gear and took off back for the girl's house to drop her off. And when she got out of the car, what do you think she saw?"

"What?" breathed Julie.

"A *hook* hanging from the door handle!"

"Ooh!"

"Well, I heard Sister McCullers telling Sister Bradford there might be some bad men roaming the woods at night," I said, not only because it was true but also because I was feeling perverse again and wanted to instigate a little adrenalin flow. "That we ought to be real careful if we have to get up to go to the latrine after dark."

"Do you really think there'll be any trouble, Diana?" asked Hannah. "My mom only let me come because the bishop promised her we'd be okay."

"The Church would never do anything that put us in real danger," I replied, trying not to sound regretful. Perhaps a mission to Brazil, though, might pose *some* adventure. And we had all heard about those missionaries kidnapped by evil men in Russia. "Besides, Sister Bradford brought a gun."

"A gun! How do you know?"

"She showed it to me. She told me not to tell anyone. But you guys aren't 'anyone.'"

We talked for another twenty or thirty minutes, but as it had been a long day, we eventually nodded off one after the other. I dreamed about finding a cure for Ebola and then waking up worried I might have diarrhea out here in the middle of nowhere. Or that some of the girls would have their periods and spread disease among the entire group. I was nothing if not morbid.

Looking up at the stars at night, I began to wonder whether with such disease all over the world if there was even a God out there to begin with. Perverse. But hopefully, involving myself fully in these church activities would salvage my soul.

We held Seminary scripture chases during lunch each day. I knew almost all the answers. But knowing the answers didn't mean I didn't still have questions. I tried to throw myself into the physicality of the entire experience, hoping that would help, too.

By the end of the fifth day, even hiking and swimming began to grow tedious. I could see that even the adults were ready for the week to be over. I lazily scratched at my own mosquito bites as we started to eat. Not being an idiot, of course, I didn't have any poison ivy to worry about. I tried to psyche myself up for another painful evening of Church history.

Halfway through dinner, though, everything changed.

Brother Campbell came running into the camp. We hadn't even noticed he was gone. "Everyone, get up!" he shouted.

"What is it?" Sister Bradford demanded.

"There's an anti-Mormon mob heading this way! They're going to rape all the girls and kill us because we're Mormon!"

The girls all jumped up, their food spilling everywhere. Hannah grabbed my hand.

"I'll go try to head them off!" shouted Brother Campbell, heading back the way he'd come.

"Come on!" Sister Bradford said authoritatively. "We're going to run up the trail and hide."

"But it's dark out there," whined one of the girls.

"Everyone get their flashlights," Sister Bradford ordered. She went to her own tent and came back with her gun. Hannah squeezed my hand harder.

Within five minutes, we'd abandoned camp. One of the leaders tried to call 9-1-1 but couldn't get a signal. We took off up the trail, huffing because of the incline. After twenty minutes, we came to a small clearing. The sisters gathered us around them, made us call out our names, and then ordered us to turn off the flashlights.

There was only a tiny sliver of moon, and everything went black.

"I'm scared," said Julie.

"Diana, what are we going to do?" asked Hannah.

"The Lord will take care of us," I said. I didn't know what was going to happen out here, but I knew I wanted Hannah not to feel afraid.

"Do you really think so?" asked Connie. "I mean, even Mormons die sometimes."

Julie started crying.

I knew I didn't want to die for a religion I wasn't even sure I believed.

"Everyone, hush!" whispered Sister Bradford loudly. "Don't make a peep! If that mob is looking for us, we don't want to give ourselves away. Stay absolutely quiet until I give the word."

We all held hands, standing, afraid to sit. The fear was contagious and kept us from growing tired, even after another twenty minutes had passed. Then we heard it—steps coming along the trail. Lots of steps.

"Shhh!" whispered Sister Bradford. But I could still hear one of the girls sniffling.

After a while, the sound of footsteps dissipated, and another fifteen minutes after that, Sister Bradford turned on her flashlight. "You, Diana," she said.

"Yes?"

"You and I are going back to the camp to see if it's safe to return." She held the flashlight in one hand and her gun in the other. "The rest of you stay here in the dark. And keep quiet."

Hannah grabbed for me. "Don't go, Diana!"

I kissed her on the mouth and then walked over to join Sister Bradford. I felt sorry for my parents. The news was going to be so hard on them. I felt sorry for Hannah, too. She was never going to have another friend who loved her like I did.

And I felt mad at the bishop and the stake president. Weren't they supposed to be inspired?

Sister Bradford and I walked carefully down to the camp and looked about. Even the one flashlight didn't provide much illumination, and she wouldn't let me turn mine on, afraid the extra light would give us away. We paused several times along the way and then kept going. The camp was deserted and showed no signs of anyone having been there besides us. After looking into each tent and determining everything looked okay, we walked quickly back up the trail. This time, I was allowed to turn on my beam.

When we reached the group, Hannah grabbed me and buried her face in my neck. Several of the other girls were crying audibly in relief. Sister Bradford ordered everyone to turn on their flashlights. Turning her own upward to light her face from below, she started talking.

"Okay, girls, you can all relax now. There is no anti-Mormon mob. We just wanted you to feel what it means to be Mormon in a world that hates us. We're always under attack in one way or another, and the threat of real anti-Mormon mobs is just one new state or federal law away."

The girls stopped crying and stared at her. Hannah was still holding onto my hand tightly. As I listened to the unbelievable words, I realized I was squeezing hers tightly as well.

"We're always being threatened because of our beliefs," Sister Bradford went on, "and the only way we can be prepared for whatever might happen is by having strong testimonies." She smiled, but because of the way the lighting from below struck her face, it made her grin look macabre. "So let's spend the next hour bearing our testimonies here in this clearing before we head back to camp."

"I'll start," said Sister Goodson. She began bearing her testimony of the truthfulness of the gospel. As I looked about me, I realized that testimonies were contagious, too. And these women knew that.

"I—I don't understand," Hannah whispered to me.

"They were lying," I replied. They must have had some of the priesthood come out to scare us with the footsteps.

"But that's—that's mean," she said.

"Let's make our way to the edge of the crowd," I whispered. "Then we'll sneak away and head back to the camp. Give them a little scare of their own when they realize we're missing."

"What'll we do back at camp all alone?" she asked.

"We'll eat the rest of our dinner and go to bed. I'm exhausted."

We made our way back down the trail. There were enough embers in the pit to get the fire going again, and we finished our interrupted meal. I could see streaks on Hannah's face where her tears had cleared some of the dust and dirt from the last few days away. Looking at her, I suddenly felt very sad. I wouldn't be seeing her much anymore, as I'd no longer be going to church, while I knew she would. I felt sorry for my parents, too, who would never understand why I couldn't go back.

Hannah and I cleaned up our dinner things and then crawled into our tent. I held her hand as she quickly fell asleep and kept holding onto it tightly even after I heard the heavy sound of footsteps coming back loudly down the trail.

The Endoscopy Party

Lindsay walked slowly up to the house listed on the invitation, hoping the neighbors didn't know about the party. She could hardly believe she was attending. An endoscopy party, for goodness' sake. Someone at her clinic had hung around the waiting room for three days, asking extremely personal questions, to get a list of twenty-five people who were having endoscopies, so he could invite them all to a party.

Lindsay had thought he was a freak, but then he'd said, "I can see you blushing. That's exactly why we need to socialize. So we can see this is no different than a teeth cleaning or irrigating the wax out of your ears."

Well, both of *those* things were disgusting, too.

Lindsay knocked timidly on the door. No one answered, but she could hear lots of talking inside, so she turned the handle gingerly and pushed open the door. In the living room were several men and women, holding drinks in plastic cups and eating food off paper plates as they mingled.

A man about thirty-five looked in Lindsay's direction and she felt her face burn. She forced a smile and made her way through the crowd, trying to find Saul, the host. She found him in the dining room, placing a bowl of fried rice on a table. Lindsay experienced a flash of horror as she realized this was a potluck and she hadn't brought anything. She hadn't planned to come at all, only deciding at the last minute to give it a try, and preparing a dish had completely escaped her mind. She blushed again.

"S-Saul," she stammered, "I'm sorry I didn't bring anything."

Saul reached over and hugged her. "You brought yourself. That's all that matters."

Lindsay felt completely stupid. She knew her company wasn't worth much in the best of times, much less at a party like this. These people weren't even Mormons. All she had in common with them was that she'd had a hose put up her butt. Maybe she should just leave.

"Hi," said a woman about fifty, at least twenty years older than Lindsay. "Polyps. How about you?"

"Oh, I—I'd rather not say."

The woman laughed. "You been through as many vaginal exams as I have, a few polyps don't embarrass you. I'm Jessica."

"Lindsay."

"Try the jalapeno bread. It's good."

Lindsay couldn't afford to eat bread. She was easily thirty-five pounds overweight, one of the girls the guys felt obliged to dance with once at each Single Adults dance, out of charity. She was embarrassed every time she walked into the chapel on Sunday still single, embarrassed that it was because she was fat, embarrassed that even being single, she still hadn't gone on a mission.

"So, what do you do?" Jessica asked.

"I'm a cleaning lady," said Lindsay, jutting out her chin a little. "In an office downtown."

"How nice."

Lindsay remembered her manners. "And you?"

Jessica smiled. "I'm an attorney."

"Sounds like a personal problem," said a man about forty, leaning in. "Hi, I'm Fred."

Jessica moved on, and Lindsay smiled uncertainly. She was never any good at parties, always a wallflower. Even at Single Adult Family Home Evening, where she knew everybody, she still hardly said a word. "Polyps?" she asked, with no idea why she'd said such a thing.

"Just a check-up. My father died of colon cancer."

"Oh, I'm sorry."

"If you had a choice between breast cancer and waving your tits at your boss, which would you choose?"

"Pardon me?"

"If you could prevent breast cancer just by a few minutes of embarrassment, wouldn't it be worth it?"

Lindsay thought for a second. She didn't even give herself a manual breast exam, much less go in for a check-up. She was a little young for breast cancer, but why did she feel she couldn't ever touch herself? It wasn't as if a breast self-exam were masturbation.

"I suppose so," she said.

"Then why is everyone afraid of a colon exam?"

Lindsay frowned. Her ass simply felt more vulnerable than her breasts, and even then, she *wouldn't* flash her breasts at just anyone in the first place.

"It's not as if there's any shit involved," said Fred. "You're completely cleaned out before the exam."

"I think I see someone I know." Lindsay smiled and crossed the room. What in the world was she doing here? Were people really going to talk about all of this in public, and while they were eating? What was wrong with them? Maybe she'd stay just a few more minutes and then skip out.

"Hi, I'm Lindsay." Lindsay would not normally have been so brazen, but she had to talk to someone or Fred would know she'd simply dumped him.

"Winona. Polyps?"

Oh my god.

Lindsay forced a smile, and Winona handed her a bottle of red wine. "The wine's good," she said. "I picked it out myself. Have some."

"Oh, no thank you. I don't drink."

Winona suddenly looked disgusted. "That's just what my kids say. A real bunch of party-poopers. You know, when they were little, they used to sneak in my dope box and steal my dope, but now they want to be perfect little angels. Makes me sick. Who are they trying to impress?"

Lindsay reddened, knowing the criticism was directed at her as well. But she was trying to impress Heavenly Father, of course. He'd forbidden such things. He forbid a lot of things, and he commanded, "Be ye therefore perfect." Every sin and flaw and weakness was another thing to be ashamed of. Even feeling bad that she wasn't impressing Winona somehow seemed a failure.

"Are you trying to be a good girl?" Winona asked in a condescending tone.

What an ass. "Yes, I am." That was one thing Lindsay wasn't ashamed of. Only she could feel the blood rush to her face anyway.

Lindsay turned away and picked up a plate. She put some paté on a cracker. It looked good but tasted awful. And she scooped up some potato salad. It didn't look particularly good but actually wasn't bad. Then she spooned some mixed green salad onto her plate. It looked good but had bleu cheese dressing and tasted nasty.

How could people like mold, thought Lindsay. But she liked cheddar, didn't she, and brie and mozzarella. All those were made from contaminated milk, too.

Lindsay found a chair out on the back patio and sat down. She'd finish eating and go home. Why was she even trying to socialize outside of gospel circles anyway? That kind of behavior never led to anything good. If she were a better person, she could ask the Golden Questions and get a referral for the missionaries, but she was far too embarrassed to do that.

Lindsay looked at the people milling about her. In some ways, they didn't quite seem human. She knew that was small-minded of her, but how could someone who didn't know the Plan of Salvation really be fully human? In so many ways, those people were like animals. You had to be nice to animals, too, of course, but just as you could never truly communicate with a cat, you could also never fully communicate with someone who didn't understand temple rites.

Lindsay frowned. *She* didn't understand temple rites, either. They mystified her. Her bishop had wanted her to wait till she went on a mission or got married before she went through the temple, but Lindsay felt that was an unnecessary deprivation. So she went to the temple every couple of months. She always volunteered for the prayer circle, fantasizing she might meet her future husband there, holding her hand in the secret handshake.

She always went home feeling more alone than ever.

"Mind if I sit down?"

Lindsay glanced up and saw the man about thirty-five who'd looked at her when she first came in. He was clean-shaven and relatively handsome. What could he want with her? Maybe he was simply tired of standing. "Oh, sure, go ahead."

"My name's Tom." He offered his hand while holding his plate with the other.

"Lindsay."

"Pretty name."

"Thanks."

"Irritable Bowel Syndrome?" he asked.

"Huh?"

"Crohn's Disease?"

"Uh…"

"You look too young to be worried about cancer."

Lindsay wanted to say something completely outrageous. "I had a dream I needed a check-up. A vision."

Tom's eyebrows lifted. "You're a visionary?"

Lindsay had lots of dreams she thought were meaningful, but the only one that had ever come true was the one when she lost a favorite earring. She dreamed it was at a restaurant where she'd eaten two days earlier, and sure enough, when she went to go see, the owner had it in Lost and Found. "I believe God tells us things," she said.

Tom nodded. "I used to be a Catholic priest," he said slowly. "But I was asked to leave because I kept going to see my psychic advisor, and they thought it looked bad."

Lindsay stared at him. It made sense really, she thought. Without the gospel, you'd be grasping at straws. There were people happy with what the Catholic Church taught them, or what their astrologer said, or what some science fiction writer taught, but Lindsay wondered if being happy was good if it was all based on an illusion.

The more Lindsay thought about the Book of Mormon, though, the more she wondered if Joseph Smith wasn't simply the fantasy writer of his time. Very little that was known of Native Americans seemed to suggest a DNA source out of Jerusalem, or a language based on reformed Egyptian. No city of Zarahemla had ever been found. All the stories in the Book of Mormon seemed to take place in Central America, so why did the plates get buried in upstate New York? Lindsay was trying so hard to be a good Mormon girl, but there was something hidden deep inside her, lurking unseen, ready to cause disaster at any moment.

What if it was all a lie?

"Try the bean dip," Tom suggested, pointing.

"Oh, I don't know," Lindsay replied, looking at the card table set up outside in confusion.

"So what if you get gas? It's an endoscopy party. Live dangerously."

He smiled, stood up to dunk a Dorito in the dip, and walked off, winking at her.

Tom was certainly cute, Lindsay thought, but he was also off limits since he wasn't LDS. It just felt unfair to be limited to guys who didn't seem to like her. Tom was at least nice. She could be friends with him, couldn't she, and if nothing ever clicked, he still might have other friends who might be interested. He'd been willing to live a life of celibacy, but

Lindsay wasn't sure she was. And she wasn't getting any prettier.

She watched as Tom continued mingling, talking first with a man about sixty and then to a woman about forty-five. She wondered now if maybe this wasn't the reason she'd talked herself into attending in the first place. The Single Adult group at church was always going to keep her single.

But could she do something as daring as go out with a non-member? It might be the first step on the road to apostasy.

She would stay just ten more minutes. If Tom came back and talked to her during that time, she would go out with him.

Lindsay stood up and moved over to a picnic bench where three people were sitting, two women and one man. She smiled brightly, hoping Tom could see how friendly she was, and nodded at one of the women. "I'm Lindsay," she said.

"Allison," said the woman. "And this is my partner, Shirley." The other woman waved.

"Oh, hi."

"Allison was just telling us how hard it is to keep Shirley in the country," the man offered. "Shirley's from South Africa and can't get a green card. And of course, since they can't get married…"

Lindsay had never thought all that much about gay people, or lesbians, either, but it suddenly struck her as horrific to have somehow been able to find a person you liked in this world where people were so particular, and then not be able to be with them.

They talked for a few more minutes, and then another woman, around sixty, joined them. "You know, I couldn't even tell my husband where I was the day I had my procedure. We're supposed to have someone drive us home, and I had to get my neighbor. Ellis is mortified if I hear him farting. He'd die before he had an endoscopy. Literally."

It was getting easier to hear this kind of talk, Lindsay realized, but she wondered if that was a good thing. Even if *she* were able to accept all bodily functions without shame, almost no one else she'd be talking to at church or at work would be able to, so what good did her superior wisdom do her?

It wasn't unlike being a Mormon. No one wanted to hear about that, either, and people grew instantly uncomfortable if the topic were raised.

But then, maybe telling a Catholic that everything they'd believed their whole life was rubbish really was a shitty thing to say.

Perhaps she should talk to Tom just to listen to someone else's point of view for a change.

The sixty-year-old spoke again. "Once, maybe twenty years ago, Ellis farted right when he came. He was so upset he wouldn't have sex for two months. I ended up inviting the mailman in one day. That mailman stopped in twice a week for the next five years, till they changed his route."

"Did your husband ever find out?" Allison asked.

"I never told him." She shrugged. "I wasn't ashamed. I just knew there are some things best not talked about."

"I'm a cutter," said Shirley.

"What's that?"

"I sometimes take a knife and cut myself. It's comforting for some reason."

"And I'm schizophrenic," said the man at the table, "but I take my meds."

Why were *all* these people talking about things best not talked about, thought Lindsay. Or did everyone have an elephant in the living room?

She suddenly grew very envious. These people might have their problems, and problems always felt so confining to Lindsay, but these people somehow seemed free. She always strived to be perfect, but was repression the same thing as perfection?

A man joined the group and began talking about his long-haired dachshund. Lindsay was mildly interested but then started worrying that Tom might leave the party before she had a chance to talk to him again. She just had to go out with him at least once, have a cup of coffee, or maybe really be daring and have a glass of wine.

Maybe…maybe she'd even try to have sex. She remembered the time last month when she was feeling antsy and she'd rented the movie *Saw*. It had been terribly decadent of her, but she was amazed at how liberating it had felt. And she couldn't help but wonder if perhaps the Church weren't a bit like the terrible character in the movie, just creating elaborate traps for people who wandered innocently into their grasp.

She'd fasted on a regular Sunday to make up for the sin and tried not to doubt anymore, but then she'd been bold and accepted this invitation. She didn't want to leave without giving someone her phone number. She glanced around but couldn't see Tom. Had he gone back inside, or had he left?

"How about you?" asked the man.

"Excuse me?"

"You have any pets?"

"Oh," said Lindsay. This seemed like the kind of lame topic *she* would normally have chosen, and it irritated her that she had nothing interesting to say. "I have a cat." She paused. "I love her but feeding her gets expensive."

"Cat food is expensive?" Allison asked.

"Well, she eats palm trees," Lindsay explained. "Every two weeks, I buy her a baby ponytail palm. It has to be just the right age to have the crunchiness and taste she likes, but she really looks forward to her palm trees."

Everyone laughed, and Lindsay felt a little surprised. No one ever considered her entertaining. Of course, no one usually asked her any questions.

"In fact," she went on, deciding to extend her attempt at a daring life a few moments longer, "the supplier at my nursery noticed how many more ponytail palms they were selling and thought the plant had finally become popular. When the nursery owner told them it was only me, they were disappointed. But they did write it up in their newsletter, trying to get more cat owners interested."

Everyone laughed again, and Lindsay smiled.

"You're charming."

Lindsay turned to look. It was Tom, who'd slipped in unnoticed. He took her elbow and led her away from the others. "Would you like to go out sometime?" he asked.

Lindsay nodded, and Tom smiled. Then he grew serious again. "There's something I have to tell you first."

Lindsay looked at him expectantly.

"I've learned when dating you have to be upfront about certain things." He paused slightly. "If you have HIV, you have to say it at the beginning. If you have herpes, you have to let your partner know."

Lindsay knew she should be horrified to hear all this. Dating outside the Church was certainly going to be challenging. But somehow, she didn't care.

"And you?" she asked. "You...?" She didn't even know enough to know what to ask.

"I like women," Tom said softly, "but I only like to have anal sex. Would you be up for that?"

How forward he was being. How presumptuous. How...how worldly. She should feel offended and mortified and, well, ashamed, but she nodded slowly. "I'd love to have you inside my ass," she said. Why wasn't her face burning when she said such things?

Tom smiled. "I like to be pegged, too."

She had absolutely no clue what he was talking about but figured she'd find out in time.

"Normally, I'd like to wait till the *end* of a date to suggest this, but why don't we have sex now? We're at an endoscopy party, after all. It somehow seems fitting. Let's go slip in the bathroom."

Lindsay had heard about guys who were only after sex, but this didn't feel like that. And yet, even if Tom didn't want to go out after they'd visited in the bathroom, she could live with that as well. "You go in first," she said, "and I'll come in right after."

They went inside the house and put their plates down. They meandered through the rooms till they came upon the bathroom. Tom smiled at her and calmly walked inside. Watching the door close, Lindsay took a deep breath. This was it. No more temple rites. No more church dances. No more Single Adult Family Home Evenings. She breathed out.

And no more shame for not being perfect. No more shame for all the things that were just a natural part of who she was. She felt she'd just had a polyp removed.

This was the reason she'd come to the party, though, and she was going to grab the opportunity. Sometimes, you just had to clean the tissue and make an incision.

Lindsay wondered if it would take very long to heal.

She smiled and pushed open the door.

Granny's Secret Vice

"Now you be a good girl and go watch some television. Granny needs some time to herself for a while."

"Granny, I'm thirteen years old," I said. "Don't treat me like a child."

"Okay, Faith, okay. Go masturbate for a bit. I need some time to myself."

I was long past being shocked at things Granny might say. She was a Democrat, for one thing, and subscribed to *Sunstone* magazine for another. Gramps had been a Republican, of course, and they'd nevertheless managed to get along well, up until the day he'd been gored to death by a mountain goat in Olympic National Park on his 68th birthday.

That was a long time ago, a year before I was born, but every year on his birthday, Granny still hiked up the trail where he'd been killed. I was never quite sure she wasn't going up to gloat. Dad said Granny had always told Gramps that God favored liberals. Last year when Granny had had me watch *Auntie Mame* with her, I was struck by the similarity of her reaction with Auntie Mame's when her husband died on a mountain, too. And Granny wouldn't tolerate a single word around the kitchen table that hinted at prejudice, even against people like Mexicans or drug abusers.

Just last night, she'd said, "Are you so sure *you* would never use drugs if your mother was a drunk, you were poor, not interested in school, and all your friends were using?"

"So you're saying that drug users are losers anyway, even if they don't abuse drugs?"

"Touché," she'd said, laughing. "You caught me on my own stereotype. Good job."

Granny's greatest failing, in my opinion, was that she was always trying to "teach." I tried to forgive her, knowing education had been her lifelong career. But it could sure get annoying.

I watched now as Granny closed her bedroom door, and I heard the click of the lock. I went over to the door and tried to listen. I heard another click and then a squeak. Granny was opening the chest she kept at the foot of her bed. My older brother Will and I had tried to get inside that chest for years. Granny refused to tell us what was in it, but we knew it was something important. She always locked her bedroom door before opening it.

I wished Will were here. We fought sometimes, but now that he was a senior in high school, he seemed to have matured a bit and wasn't nearly the brat he used to be. I alone was visiting Granny on Thanksgiving break, however. The rest of the family was visiting Mom's parents.

Although they were temple workers, I always found them a little too artificially sweet, like Splenda, and I was afraid some unnatural chemical reaction was taking place inside me when I was with them. Granny, though, when she said, "For God's sake, one cup of coffee isn't going to kill you," made me feel at home.

Not that we ever drank coffee at home. We weren't even allowed to drink Coke. But I liked living on the edge. And when I discovered I'd be alone with Granny for four days if I insisted on coming, I insisted.

I walked over to the TV and turned it on. Jerry Springer flashed on the screen. Masturbating would be less decadent.

I thought about my grandmother's comment. I of course had never touched myself inappropriately, but I'd certainly thought about boys. My parents were sticklers for the rules, so I wouldn't be allowed to date until I was sixteen. I might just *have* to take Granny's counsel eventually.

Granny hadn't married until she was thirty-four, and she freely admitted she hadn't been a virgin. Still, she told me she hadn't explained that to the bishop, so she and Gramps had gone ahead and married in the temple. "God understands human desire," she said. "He gave us desire, after all."

I wondered if there was a statute of limitations on sin. If you never officially repented, did the sin still expire at some point?

I flipped channels. Judge Judy. Judge Joe Brown. Judge Hatchett. Sheesh. Why did people like judges so much?

I turned off the TV and picked up *Sunstone*. Some boring article about Joseph Smith's First Vision. Bleah. And an article about the need for civil discourse. Slightly more intriguing. I was going to be a Republican like the rest of my family, but I had to admit, some of the things I heard on Fox

News made me uncomfortable. Democrats like Granny might be sinners, but that didn't mean we shouldn't still love them.

Dad always said you could only trust the handshake of a Republican, but I wasn't sure that statement was any more trustworthy than something Obama might say. Dad wouldn't even shake hands with people at church if he saw they hadn't taken the sacrament. He was always afraid to touch anyone he thought had sinned. This obviously meant I kept a lot of personal information back, though I guess I was a good enough girl in most respects. He didn't need to know I sometimes sent emails to the President asking him to end the war.

When I heard the bedroom door open and saw Granny walking toward me with a smile, I asked, "Feel better now?" I paused and tried to sound casual. "Did you wash off your dildo?" Sometimes, I knew I was terrible.

"Faith! I swear! Where do you get the nerve to talk like that?" But she was smiling.

"From you, Granny." I batted my eyes innocently.

"Well, the answer is no. I use a condom on my dildo, so cleaning up is much easier."

She smiled again, and I couldn't tell if she was joking or not. I'd certainly never have said such outrageous things if my family were present, but talking so sinfully when we were alone together was like having a private secret. And secrets made people feel special.

"Are you ever going to tell me what you have locked up in that trunk?"

"Perhaps." Granny shrugged. "You'll have to prove yourself first. Gramps never did. Nor did your father. Will is out of the question. But you, well, there's hope for you."

"What do I have to do?"

"Oh, I can't tell you. It has to come naturally or there's no point."

Well, I already said terrible things around Granny, so that couldn't be it. I drank coffee when I was alone with her. We watched forbidden R-rated movies together. What more could she want?

"Tell me another story from when you were young," I said. Perhaps that would give me a clue.

Granny shrugged again. "I was teaching elementary school when I was twenty. And I liked it well enough. But after a few years, I decided to get a Master's and become a principal. I can tell you, there weren't many women in graduate school back then."

"Well, *I* plan to go to graduate school," I said.

Granny smiled. "What will you study?"

"I—I don't know," I admitted. "But something *important*."

"I certainly hope so, dear."

Should I have lied and said medicine or physics? I was sure Granny would see through any subterfuge. All I really liked was art, and there was obviously no future in that.

"What should we do before you cook me dinner?" Granny asked.

"Children are supposed to grow up loving their grandmother's cooking," I said. "Why do you have *me* cook every day?"

"I cooked the turkey, didn't I?"

"Yes, but…"

"Life is community working together."

Part of me resented having an odd grandmother. "You could at least teach me one of your favorite recipes."

"My favorites are all marked in the cookbooks."

"Surely, you have some secret ingredients."

Granny shrugged.

"Sheesh, Granny."

"It's 'Jesus, Granny.'"

"Oh, for God's sake."

"That's better."

She pulled out the Scrabble board and we began playing, as we did every afternoon. I was happy to come up with "truck" and even happier when I turned Granny's "fast" to "fasten." But she then turned it into "fastener" and changed my simple "cut" to "cuticle." She was a master.

"What's your favorite subject at school?" Granny asked.

It was band, another field which held no future. But I said, "English," since I knew that was Granny's specialty.

"Liar."

"How do you know?"

"Because you haven't picked up a single book since you got here."

"Well, that's because I want to spend time with *you*."

She waved the comment aside. "So what's your favorite subject?"

I sighed. "Band. I love playing the French horn."

Granny grunted. "Do you like classical music?"

I shrugged. "Not to listen to. I like Miley Cyrus. But I love *playing* classical music. It's fun."

Granny grunted again. "You like it enough to do eight hours a day?"

I frowned. "I don't know if I like *anything* well enough to do eight hours a day."

Granny laughed at that, and I smiled, though I'd been completely serious. I'd never made it through an eight-hour movie marathon. Even amusement parks grew exhausting after eight hours. I did think maybe I could draw for eight hours straight. I'd done that before on a Saturday when I didn't have anything else planned. But that seemed even flightier than playing the French horn, and I was too embarrassed to bring it up.

Then again, even the best art museums got boring well before the eight-hour mark.

Swimming?

Lying on the beach?

I looked over at Granny. Perhaps masturbating?

I sure didn't want to make a living at that!

"What was your favorite thing to do when you were my age?" I asked.

"Oh, that's the secret, isn't it?" she said, shaking her head. "What I enjoyed at thirteen I still enjoy today. Behind closed doors."

"Granny, *do* you really masturbate?"

She laughed. "Well, you get a point for asking, anyway."

We talked of other things then. Granny explained why it was important to protect Social Security, and why public education was more important to support than private schooling, and why it was a moral imperative to provide universal healthcare. I smiled politely as she talked, but none of it seemed particularly important to me. When was *I* ever going to need any of that?

Still, I asked about gay rights and climate change and legalizing marijuana because I worried that Granny was going to hell. She *sounded* compassionate when she talked of these things, but wasn't she just being deceived? Sometimes, I thought of her as belonging to another species, she was so different from the rest of the family. There were times I was a little afraid even to touch her. And yet there were moments I wondered about a few of the "big issues." Even now, I started staring off into space.

"What's on your mind?"

"I know Mormons are supposed to know all the answers, but sometimes…"

"Yes?"

I was silent a moment. I wanted to be on Granny's side, but weren't some things beyond the pale? "How can you be a Democrat, Granny? Democrats believe in abortion."

"So?"

"You can't possibly support that. Not as a Latter-day Saint."

Granny gave me a long, silent, appraising look. I felt my face burning, but I looked back at her boldly. "Young lady," she said slowly, "I had a back alley abortion after I was raped by my uncle when I was only two years older than you are now. He arranged for the doctor. The only good thing that bastard ever did. But it's why I was only able to have one child later. I was lucky even to have your father." She paused. "If you can call that luck."

I stared, unable to speak. Finally, I managed, "But— but—"

"Now, don't go telling your father. He doesn't know a thing about it. This is just between us girls."

I nodded but didn't say anything. I simply didn't know what to think. If abortion was murder, then killing an innocent baby just because *you* were wronged was unjustifiable, too. And yet, having a baby at fifteen back in 1945 would have destroyed Granny's life forever. Still, to have a difficult and unhappy life didn't justify murder, either. I always knew Granny was radical, but this might be going too far.

Granny must have sensed my doubts, because a moment later, she said softly, "How would you feel if Will raped you?"

"He would never!" I said.

"That's how I felt about my favorite uncle. He was a bishop at the time, too."

I wasn't sure I even believed her anymore. I was frowning when she suddenly reached over and pinched my arm.

"Ow!"

"I am not a machine, you know. I don't simply follow my computer chip and knit blankets and bake cookies. I am a human being, just like you."

I rubbed my arm, still frowning, but more confused than ever. I'd always known Granny to be a sinner, and yet…she was certainly no robot.

"What makes people do bad things?" I asked.

"Bad like having abortions?"

"Bad like…raping their niece."

Granny sighed. "That was the big question in my life." She laughed, and I began to understand what the word bitter might mean. "In my day, people thought it was comic books that made boys bad."

"You can't be serious."

"Sure, just like people blame computer games today."

I thought about it.

"I already liked comics myself, but at fifteen, I started sneaking more of them into the house. And when I was a teacher a few years later, I used to confiscate the comic books my students brought to class and stay up all night reading them."

"And were they bad?" I asked.

"I *loved* them," she said, laughing again, not so bitterly this time.

I laughed, too. "Well, I like this comic book called *Wormwood*," I said, immediately feeling uncomfortable, knowing my dad would kill me if Granny said anything and he ever took a look at it. "I—I've even drawn my own stories for it." Then I bit my lip, realizing I'd really said too much now.

"You draw comics?" Granny asked, frowning at this news.

"Y-yes," I said. If she was going to tell her secret about the rape, then I could be brave and tell mine as well. "I want to be a comic book artist. Write graphic novels. *That's* what I enjoy doing for eight hours."

Granny stared at me as if seeing me for the first time. I felt decidedly uneasy, and I realized that all secrets were not equal. A smoker could condemn a drinker. A drinker could condemn someone for being overweight. An overweight woman could condemn a…a Democrat. There were many levels of judgment, and everyone always felt *they* were on the right side of the bar.

"Well, I'll be."

"You won't tell Dad, will you?"

"What kind of art education do you get at your fancy private school?"

I shrugged. "Not much really. We focus more on English and math."

"Those are certainly good things to focus on."

"But there's this art institute in Chicago I'd like to attend after I graduate. I'm saving up lunch money."

"Lunch money?"

"I figure if I'm going to be anorexic, I may as well get something out of it."

"You *are* a little too thin. Do you really save your lunch money?"

"Yes. And I just started babysitting, so I save all that, too. Except for the ten percent I give to the Church."

"Uh-huh."

There was a moment or two of awkward silence between us, and I looked at my lap. "Do you think it's a silly dream?" I asked in a small voice.

"Well, of *course* it's a silly dream," Granny said, slapping my leg. "Those are the only kind worth having."

"You don't think I should study law or chemistry or something?"

"Those would be great dreams, too. But you have to follow the one that's yours."

"What if no one likes my art?"

"What if you're a lawyer and you work with judges who rule against you?"

"Huh?"

"There are dangers in every profession."

"Even being a principal?"

Granny laughed. "Are you kidding me?"

"Maybe—maybe I'll show you one of my drawings sometime."

Granny stood up and walked to a drawer in the kitchen. She came back with a blank piece of paper. "Let's see what you got."

"Draw here? With you watching?"

"Life is all about performance under pressure." She brought me a pencil, and I began drawing one of my favorite characters from *Wormwood*. In just a few minutes, I had a scene starting to materialize. Granny pushed me aside and stared at the paper.

"Yep," she said. "You can do it."

"You really think so?"

"Do you know what my Master's thesis was in graduate school?"

"No."

"The effects of comic books on the male juvenile mind."

I giggled.

"My professors didn't even want to accept it. But my research was sound."

"And did comics really have no effect at all?"

"Boys tend to get in trouble regardless. You can be Catholic and bad, or Baptist and bad, or Mormon and bad, or a comic book reader and bad. I found that the overall environment, primarily the family and neighborhood, had far more influence on character than a mere comic book."

"So family is important, just like the Church says."

"Certainly, it's important. But Mormons don't have a monopoly on families, you know."

"Yes, but..."

"Or on incest."

I shut up. I watched a moment as Granny admired my drawing, but I finally had to speak again. "Do you not even believe the Church is true?" I asked.

Granny didn't say anything right away. Then she looked at me carefully. "What did you think of *The Accused* last night?"

"Well, to be honest, Granny, it made me uncomfortable."

"Why is that?"

"Because Jodie Foster is white trash. And yet…"

"And yet…?"

"Well, she still didn't deserve to be raped."

Granny nodded. "And do you think that's a valid lesson to learn?"

I frowned.

"The Church says you should never see that movie. How about *Midnight Cowboy* the other night?"

"Well, really, it was a little boring, but I don't suppose it was too awful to see."

"Do you know that movie originally had an X rating?"

"Oh my God!"

"Thatta girl." She smiled. "Look, the Church is fine. Lots of great stuff there. But it's a small, small world. And the real world is very, very big."

"But do you *believe*?" I pressed.

Granny shrugged. "Sometimes. But I learned a long time ago that people have an innate ability to believe all sorts of things that aren't true. Even me." She stared off toward the window. "But I try to believe things that make my world larger."

I wanted a world that *Wormwood* fit into, and that Granny fit into as well. "Are you ever going to tell me your secret?" I asked.

"I already told you."

"The rape?"

Granny stood and waved at me to follow. We walked to the bedroom and she locked the door behind us. Then she took a key from behind one of her books and walked over to the chest. My heart started beating faster. Was my great uncle mummified in there? Was there a voodoo doll she used to torment his spirit? Had she cut out his heart or cut off…something else?

Granny unlocked the chest and lifted the lid.

"Oh my God!"

"Beautiful, aren't they?"

I looked at my grandmother in amazement. "There must be a thousand of them."

"Just about. And I have a second trunk in the closet."

I laughed. "How did we ever miss that one?"

"Very often in life our focus is way too narrow, isn't it?" She smiled.

"But Granny, these must be worth a fortune."

"$14,000 the last time I checked."

I breathed out slowly.

"There's *Baffling Mysteries,*" said Granny, "and *Ghost Rider*, and *Strange Worlds*, and *Amazing Man Comics*, and *Mister Mystery*. My favorites are the *Adventures into the Unknown.*"

"They're in pretty good condition for being so old."

"That's because I treasured them even before they were worth anything. They were always valuable to me."

"I'll keep your secret, Granny," I said solemnly.

"Of course you'll keep it. And I'll change my will and leave these to you. They were going straight to charity before. But this'll pay a little toward your art education anyway."

"Oh, Granny."

We stood in silence for several minutes, just staring at the beautiful covers. "You do realize there's an ethical quandary?" she asked softly.

"What do you mean?"

"I bought most of these myself, but some of them were taken from my students. Is it fair for me to keep the profits?"

I nodded slowly. "Even if those kids would probably have lost them or thrown them away at some point anyway."

"You're thinking like a liberal now."

"How do you fix that?"

"Leave a thousand dollars of that money to the school district where I taught? Give to the poor? Donate clothes to foster children?"

I nodded again. "Some sins can't be rectified, can they?"

I noticed Granny's hand go absentmindedly to her stomach. "No, they can't. What's important is that *you* do the right thing with this money."

"Oh, please don't die until I have a comic book of my very own to show you!"

She laughed. "I'll do my best, sweetie."

I gently touched one of the covers and sighed. Then I stood up straight. "I'd better get started on dinner."

"Yes, and it's the last night we can stay up late. So I've got a four-hour R-rated movie for us. Full of sex and violence and cruelty." She grinned.

"What is it?"

"*Schindler's List.*"

I stopped short. "Oh! Damn!"

"What?"

"The whole family's coming down for Christmas. We won't have any time alone together anymore."

"Well, there's always Spring Break, isn't there?"

I smiled and took Granny's hand, and we headed slowly out to the kitchen. I pulled down a cookbook and flipped through pages until I came to a marked recipe. Then as I opened a cupboard, Granny touched my shoulder.

"Yes, Granny?" I asked.

"Call me Helen," she said.

I pulled her close and hugged her for a long, long while.

Escape from Zion

Sherman and Eudora sat watching the television in stunned silence as the announcement was made. Finally, Sherman took a deep sip of his water and said dully, "I'm so glad I had a vasectomy when I was eighteen."

Eudora put her hand on his. "And I'm so glad I had my tubes tied in college." She shook her head. "Sherman, what are we going to do? Even without kids to worry about, we're fu—" She stopped and swallowed. "We're in a lot a trouble," she corrected herself.

"It's only two and a half hours to the border from Seattle," Sherman said softly. "It's so hard to get through the checkpoints these days, but what choice do we have?"

"Oh, Sherman, we could get locked up on the spot."

"We'll be locked up soon enough anyway," he said. "What difference does it make? At least we'll have a chance."

Eudora slapped the sofa armrest. "Damn Mormons!"

"Eudora!" Sherman looked about in alarm.

"We won't even be able to pack anything, will we?" she said sadly. "We'll have to pretend it's a day trip. It's the only way we'll even have the slightest hope of getting through."

"It's not as if we have any good books we need to bring. Those were all banned years ago." Sherman laughed bitterly. "And it's not as if we've been able to keep accurate journals. We have no pot to smuggle. What's to pack?"

Eudora's shoulders slumped. "I would have liked to keep some photos. What with emails monitored, there's not even any chance of that." She sighed. "It would have been nice."

It was all so hopeless. What was the point? Then Sherman heard Eudora sniffling beside him, and he grabbed her and gave her a passionate kiss. "We're still young," he said. "Not even forty yet. Our lives aren't over. It's going to be okay."

"Oh, Sherman."

He looked at the stove, where the bacon was still sizzling. They'd been right in the middle of cooking breakfast when the announcement was made. Sherman looked at Ayla, their Australian shepherd. They'd have to leave her behind.

"Let's go," said Sherman. "Right now."

"What?"

"It's our only chance. We can only hope they haven't installed the machines on I-5 yet." Sherman walked over to the stove and turned it off. "Put on your shoes."

Ayla heard the word "shoes" and jumped up, her tail wagging. Sherman got a lump in his throat and closed his eyes. Maybe a neighbor would take the dog after they called from Canada. Unless the neighbors would be afraid to be seen doing any favors for people like them.

Damn those Mormons, Sherman echoed Eudora's words in his head. It had all started innocently enough, he recalled. A Mormon president, and a Republican Congress, as well as a Republican Supreme Court. Evangelical input interwove nicely with Mormon directives, and soon all pornography was illegal, all cursing, all sex outside of marriage, all same-sex marriage and interracial marriage, all alcohol, all tobacco, all recreational drugs, and before people could start to do anything about it, in a surprise twist, even all guns.

No abortions were allowed even to save the life of the mother. If the mother died as a result of pregnancy, she became a martyr and helped ensure her own spot in heaven.

Such a doctrine had never even been part of LDS culture before, but somehow, severity only fed more severity.

And it wasn't just the laws that were a problem. People could always break laws. But now there was no way to do that anymore, either. A research team at Brigham Young University had developed a machine that provided 100% accuracy as a lie detector.

The devices were mass produced in Utah and Idaho, all but eliminating unemployment there, and were soon required in every workplace in the country, at every workstation, at every government office disbursing benefits, at every medical clinic, anywhere someone might try to slip through the cracks.

"Have you looked at porn in the last week?"

"Have you used any curse words in the last week?"

"Have you jaywalked in the last week?"

"Have you been overpaid by a cashier in the last week and not paid the money back?"

"Have you called in sick to work when you weren't sick in the past week?"

"Have you drunk any coffee in the last week?"

Yes, coffee and tea were now illegal, too. Even evangelicals probably felt oppressed these days, but they'd gone along with too much, been paid off with the secret billions the LDS Church used to outmaneuver political rivals, and were just as trapped as everyone else.

Sherman could find no comfort in that.

The last question on the Monday morning test was always, "Have you committed any other crimes in the past week?" Some offenses merely required a fine. It was a great way to raise funds. But other crimes…

The U.S. already had the largest prison population of any country worldwide before these changes came into effect, but that population had only skyrocketed since. Private prisons now employed hundreds of thousands of people. Rehabilitation programs employed hundreds of thousands more. Mormons were going to *make* everyone be good.

Congress even passed a new law. The official name of the country was changed to Zion. Almost as an afterthought, the state of Utah became Deseret. There'd been debate for a while over whether to move the capital of the nation to Salt Lake, but it was eventually decided to relocate it to Jackson County, Missouri, and heavy building projects were underway there, employing thousands and thousands of people.

No one could say the new regime didn't have good jobs reports.

But after today's announcement, anything resembling a normal life was over. Sherman grabbed Eudora's hand and led her to the bedroom. "Don't wear your best dress," he said. "Look as plain as possible."

"But you'd better wear a white shirt," she replied.

He nodded.

They dressed quickly and put on good walking shoes, grabbing light jackets as it was early April and still a bit chilly. Sherman filled two bowls with dog food and three bowls with water and kissed Ayla on the head. She wagged her tail nervously, aware something was up but not sure what.

Sherman climbed behind the wheel of the car and looked over at Eudora. They both nodded grimly and took a deep breath. Then Sherman pulled out of the driveway. He'd miss his friends, his brothers, his parents, even some of his coworkers. But it wasn't as if anyone could have fully realized relationships in the current atmosphere anyway. Everyone was afraid of being reported. One of the test questions was always, "Are you aware of anyone *else* breaking any laws?"

Eudora turned the radio on, and they listened to choral music. It was Sunday, after all, and classical was pretty much the only music allowed on this day of the week. It set

Sherman's teeth on edge, but he could see it was calming Eudora, so he left it on.

Traffic was light. People were encouraged to go to church on Sundays, or visit family, but any other travel was frowned upon. They left the Seattle city limits, drove north past Lynnwood, north past Everett, and kept heading toward Bellingham. Just a little farther, thought Sherman. Just a little farther.

Damn. Why couldn't the Mormons leave well enough alone? Now they'd developed a machine that could read one's thoughts. It wouldn't be enough anymore not to lie. Now one would have to prove one didn't even *think* anything inappropriate. My god, how could anyone pass that kind of test?

The truth was that no one could. Such a device would only be used to target people you didn't like, to justify demoting someone or sterilizing them or confiscating their property.

Their only hope was that the authorities hadn't had time to install the new device at the border yet. If they had…

Sherman looked toward Eudora and she smiled weakly. It wasn't fair, he thought. It just wasn't fair. Eudora had brought nothing but joy to his life. What if she were doomed to spend the rest of hers in prison? Or even worse, being rehabilitated?

Please, God, please, he prayed.

Though these last few years, he'd developed only hatred for anything called God.

Then he shook his head. It wasn't God behind all this. It was men. God was still on his side. His and Eudora's. He would help.

As they drove through Bellingham, Sherman's stomach started knotting up. He really needed to use the bathroom. But he wasn't about to stop. They were going to keep going until they were safe.

Canada, he thought. It had been years since he'd been. British Columbia had almost seemed like just another U.S. state back in the old days. So much like America. He supposed Canadians would disagree, but it certainly hadn't been like going to Mexico all those years ago. The thought almost made him laugh. Conservatives had fought for so many years to keep "illegals" out of the country. After the new machines were installed, no one even tried to get in anymore. Problem solved overnight.

Unfortunately, of course, that only fed their belief they were doing the right thing.

Sherman heard Eudora move on the seat beside him and glanced over. She pointed through the windshield. "Border," she said.

The line of cars trying to get through wasn't very long. Answering questions about the reason for one's trip was too daunting. Answering random questions about any law one might have broken recently was daunting, too. No one wanted to face that test any more often than they had to.

"Stay calm," Sherman whispered. "It's going to be okay."

"I'm afraid."

"It's going to be okay."

All too soon, and not soon enough, it was their turn. Sherman rolled down his window and offered his left arm. After the officer strapped the device to it, he took out a pad and clicked on the first question. "What is your reason for leaving the country?"

"We just want to see the sights in Vancouver." That was true enough. You had to say something that was true. And Sherman and Eudora wanted nothing more than to see Vancouver today. Free Vancouver.

"How long do you plan to stay?"

"We shouldn't stay long," Sherman said. "We have a dog at home that needs us."

True as well. Ayla hadn't volunteered to be their sacrifice, of course. Sherman wondered if she felt as abandoned as every animal the religious had sacrificed on their altars throughout the ages. As abandoned as he and Eudora felt now, the new sacrifices on the current god's altar.

"Have you two had sex outside of the missionary position in the past week?" Now it was time for the random legal questions.

"Have you picked up after your dog this past week?"

"Have you promoted any Socialist causes this past week?"

As if there were any left.

"Have you littered anywhere this past week?"

They hardly even asked about murder and theft anymore. With no way to avoid capture, those crimes had dropped out of practice almost overnight. Even a theocracy offered some benefits or no one would have gone along. Sherman didn't want to go back to school shootings and homeless encampments. They were certainly safe in Seattle.

While there were few guns in Canada, there were still drugs there, still robberies, still lots of problems. *Was* he doing the right thing? He looked over at Eudora, who was staring straight ahead, concentrating and breathing shallowly.

"Thank you, sir," the officer said politely. "Could you step out of the car for a moment?"

Sherman frowned. Was this a normal part of the procedure? It had been so long he wasn't sure anymore. He opened the car door and stood up.

"Ma'am, could you step out of the car?"

Sherman's heart was racing. He should have brought a knife. Should he run for it? The border was only ten feet away. What about Eudora? Oh, God. Oh, God.

The officer lifted Sherman's right arm and injected something into it. Sherman looked over and saw that another officer was doing the same to Eudora. What was this? Sodium pentothal? He was already hooked up to a portable lie detector, wasn't he?

"The poison will take effect within forty-eight hours," the officer said calmly. "If you return before then, we'll inject you with the antidote." He smiled warmly and shook Sherman's hand. "Enjoy your stay in Vancouver."

"Th-thank you," Sherman replied. He glanced over at Eudora, and they both climbed quietly back into the car. The officers raised the metal arm blocking the road, and Sherman slowly drove through. He kept driving for another thirty minutes in silence. Then they turned a corner, and there was Vancouver. Sherman glanced over at Eudora. She was looking straight ahead and crying.

The Three Nephites Drink Eggnog

It was December 24th, cold here in Logan. The kids were out of school, I'd gotten off work at 3:00, and my wife Claire was busy making white chocolate chip cookies with macadamia nuts. "Jack and Cindy don't like macadamia nuts," I said.

Claire looked up from the bowl. "You know perfectly well who these are for, Peter."

"But there's a new Ammon this year," I pointed out. "Maybe he won't like them."

"Shhh," Claire whispered. "The kids'll hear."

"They're watching Christmas movies."

"Well, why did you have to get a new Ammon?" Claire went on. "What happened to the old one?"

I shrugged. "Just disappeared. You know how Nephites are."

"Please."

Every Christmas Eve for the past five years, we'd been hiring three actors from Salt Lake to come to the house and impersonate the Three Nephites. We'd had to replace actors a couple of times when people moved or had other commitments, explaining to the children that the Three Nephites frequently had to change appearance so people wouldn't get suspicious. I didn't hire anyone from Logan because I didn't want the kids accidentally running into any of them during the rest of the year.

I'd gotten the idea of creating the event when one of my neighbors told me he always hired a Santa to come visit his children, wanting them to experience the magic of belief. That seemed a scenario destined for disaster, in my opinion. You didn't want fifteen-year-old kids still believing in Santa.

So I decided I'd teach my children to believe in something real and started hiring the Three Nephites. I explained to the kids that after two thousand years of spreading the gospel, they no longer had families of their own and appreciated faithful Mormons who would host them on Christmas. This way they could remember the joys of family life awaiting them once the Millennium began and they were reunited with their own wives and children who'd died within a few decades of Christ's visit to the Americas.

Jack was eleven now and Cindy nine. They looked forward to the visit of Ammon, Mosiah, and Samuel as much as we did.

Claire spread out clumps of cookie dough on a metal sheet and placed them in the oven. "The rice'll be ready in twenty minutes," she said. "We'd better start the reading."

"Hey, kids," I called out. "Time to turn off the movie."

"Aw, Dad," said my son.

"Jack, go get your Book of Mormon."

"Can't Cindy read this year? She's big enough."

"You'll take turns. Cindy, get your Book of Mormon, too."

"Aw, Dad," said my daughter.

But soon the kids had brought their leatherbound Books of Mormon to the living room and were still smiling half-heartedly despite their childlike antagonism. They sat on the sofa while Claire and I sat on the love seat. "The Three Nephites will be here soon," I said. "Let's prepare by reading about them in Third Nephi. Cindy, you start with chapter 23."

"Dad, we know all this stuff. We read it every year," Cindy replied. She was trying to act as grown up as her brother. She got that from watching the child prodigies on the Disney channel.

"You still watch Rudolph every year, don't you?" I said. "You know that story, too."

"But that's for fun. This is…"

"This is for *real*."

Cindy nodded in resignation and began to read. I had Jack read chapter 24, Cindy read chapter 25, and so forth until Jack got to read the good chapter. 28. The other nine disciples asked Jesus to live a good life and then come speedily unto him in his kingdom, but the remaining three admitted they wanted to stay on Earth and live until Christ's return, so they'd have all those years to teach others about him.

"And they've been roaming the Earth for the past two thousand years," I concluded, "teaching everyone who will listen." It was the story my father had told me, and the story his father had told him. Our gospel roots went back to the mid-19ᵗʰ century. Our families had crossed the plains on foot to reach the Great Salt Lake Valley.

"How come we're the only ones who see them?" asked Jack, closing his scriptures.

"Oh, lots of other people see them," Claire returned. "Right, Peter?" She looked at me slightly panicked and then smiled at the kids. "Don't you remember Sister Anderson at church talking about the two mysterious men who changed her tire when she was stranded out in the desert?"

"And the two men who gave Sister Patton a quart of oil when she was stuck on the side of the road?" I added.

"Where was the third guy?" asked Cindy.

"They don't always have to travel together, do they?" I said. "The other one was somewhere else doing a good deed."

"But I thought they were supposed to be out preaching the gospel, not out doing good deeds," Jack mused.

That boy was sure being influenced by the cynicism of society. There was far too much negativity in the world today. That's what made arranging these visits so essential. "Doing good deeds is a way of preaching," I replied. Just like hiring men to fake their identity was, if it helped sustain belief.

They weren't faking, I corrected myself. They were pretending. The joy of Christmas was all about pretense.

I thought about the whiskey I had hidden in the garage.

"So why don't missionaries just go around doing good deeds?" Jack persisted.

"They *do*," said Claire. "They have to do two or three hours of community service every week. Some of them do more."

Jack looked unconvinced. The timer on the stove went off, signaling the rice was ready. Claire already had the link sausages cooked. She added butter, salt, and pepper to the rice and soon called us all to the table.

"Emily's parents always leave cookies and milk out for Santa," said Cindy. "Why don't we ever have the Three Nephites over for dinner?"

Because I'm already paying them a hundred bucks each for showing up, I thought, plus gas money. Developing faith in my children was costing me big time. I smiled and said casually, "They always say they have other plans. I think they visit other families in the area, too, before coming here."

Claire gave me a look. The kids were asking more and more difficult questions every year. It wouldn't be long before we'd have to stop the visits altogether, but the idea of doing so made me sad. I wished my parents had done something this wonderful for me and my brothers and sisters. The most they'd ever managed was offer their explanation for the day we'd come home and found our television, stereo, and other items missing from the house.

"Looks like the Three Nephites have stopped by," my father said with a smile. He leaned toward us kids and said conspiratorially, "I was on the bishop's list of people who could donate items if they ever moved into the neighborhood.

Isn't it nice they chose us? Think of the blessings we'll receive in heaven."

I was nine at the time, and it took me quite a while to realize my parents simply didn't want me to feel freaked out by the burglary. Even longer to understand why my father always seemed to have a headache on Sunday mornings and couldn't attend church with the rest of us. Or why my mother had so many sick days on any given day of the week.

I wasn't going to be that kind of parent to my children.

Soon dinner was over, the cookies were on the counter cooling off, and the kids were sitting anxiously on the sofa, looking at the clock on the wall.

Finally, around 7:15, there was a loud bang on the front door. I smiled. "They're here!"

"You sound like that little girl in *Poltergeist*, Dad," Jack said.

"And just who allowed you to watch such a movie?" interjected Claire. Jack shrugged. I went to open the door.

Three middle-aged men walked into the room, one of them staggering, all of them wearing blue jeans and flannel shirts, as we'd agreed. I'd long ago explained that the Three Nephites obviously couldn't dress as they had two thousand years ago if they wanted to pass in the community, but Jack in particular always turned up his nose when he saw them looking like our neighbors next door. He was still under that childish delusion that righteous people somehow looked different from everybody else.

"Ho ho ho," said the new guy, Ammon, as he bumped his way into the living room.

"You're not Santa," I hissed in his ear.

"Oh, that's right," he whispered back. I almost recoiled from the smell.

"Are you drunk?" I asked, a bit too loudly. The kids snickered.

"We had a little too much eggnog at the last house," Ammon replied with a slight slur. He winked at me.

"And just what Mormons are serving you eggnog with rum?" Claire asked with an edge to her voice. I wondered how she knew eggnog was made with rum. I at least had office Christmas parties to participate in. But then, she often commented with an odd amount of trivia on various commercials advertising vodka, hard lemonade, and that one with the suave older gentleman. Was that Dos Equis?

After Claire's question, Mosiah, a man we'd hired for three years in a row, spoke up. "Well, we visit jack-Mormons, too. Everyone needs our help these days. We even visit the bishop sometimes."

Cindy giggled, and Jack laughed outright.

"Besides," Mosiah went on, "we didn't have the Word of Wisdom back in our day. We're not really obligated the way you guys are."

I had to admit, it came in handy hiring at least one or two Mormon actors. They could culturally improvise pretty well. Still, I was angry with Ammon. I certainly wouldn't be hiring him again. He was going to ruin everything. Alcoholics made me so mad.

"Well, give us your Christmas message," I said bluntly. "We don't want to keep you."

Ammon sniffed the air. "Do I smell cookies? Perhaps a little food will counteract the eggnog."

I was surprised he could pronounce "counteract" in his condition. Or "eggnog," for that matter.

Claire stood up and walked stiffly into the kitchen and returned a moment later with a plateful of cookies. The kids each took one, both looking at the cookies disdainfully, while all three men grabbed at least two apiece. Ammon shoved the first one into his mouth and motioned for Mosiah and Samuel to say something to the kids.

Mosiah cleared his throat. "You know, children, we didn't think over here in America we'd ever get the chance to see Jesus ourselves. We knew he was born in Israel and lived over there. But just as we finally had the opportunity, you will, too, one day, and it's important to be ready for that moment. Only those of us who were prepared two thousand years ago survived all the earthquakes and other disasters and were still around for his visit. It'll be the same for you while waiting for the Second Coming. That's why you need to obey all the commandments." He smiled beatifically.

Ammon burped beside him. Samuel looked at his watch.

"Why don't you know our names?" Jack said suspiciously. "You come here every year. How come you still don't know who we are?"

Mosiah and Samuel looked at each other, and I held my breath. "You have to understand," said Mosiah. "After two thousand years meeting hundreds of new people every year, everybody's names all start to run together. Sometimes, I don't even remember *my* name." He laughed, and Claire and I forced a laugh as well. Jack looked at Cindy and frowned, but Cindy still looked enthralled by the presence of the men. I was glad she'd forgotten her earlier reticence.

"Did you bring me the book I prayed for?" Cindy asked, looking expectantly from one man to the next.

"They're not Santa's helpers," Claire reminded the kids.

Or the Great Pumpkin, I almost said out loud.

"But they're still nice guys," Cindy pointed out. "They can still give us presents."

"Young lady," I said sternly, "their coming here at all is a present." I turned back to the men. Ammon was swaying a little. Mosiah and Samuel looked decidedly uncomfortable. Mosiah cleared his throat and Samuel glanced at his watch again.

"Jesus wants you for a Sunbeam," said Mosiah.

"Oh, for Pete's sake," Jack muttered.

"Don't use my name in vain," I said. I knew just how Heavenly Father felt about things like that.

Jack rolled his eyes. Then he turned back to the Three Nephites. "I don't understand twhy you guys visit all these families on Christmas Eve. Why can't you just get married again and still have families of your own?" He looked at

Mosiah's left hand, where a wedding band was clearly visible. Mosiah saw the glance and put his hand in his pocket.

"We can concentrate better on preaching if we don't have families," he explained.

"Like Catholic priests?" asked Jack. "The apostates who forbid marriage?"

Mosiah looked at me for help. I sighed deeply and clapped my hands. "All right, everyone. The Three Nephites have a busy night. Lots of families to visit." I started ushering them to the door.

"Do you have any eggnog?" asked Ammon, bumping into the frame after I opened the door.

"We'll pray that you guys continue to have success with your preaching." Claire smiled and tried not to look irritated.

"Thanks for stopping by," I added with a wave.

Ammon had walked only three feet when he suddenly leaned over and vomited onto the walkway leading to the house. Mosiah grabbed him and pulled him away.

Pathetic. I'd tell the Salt Lake actors guild about his unprofessional appearance. Ammon wouldn't work *anywhere* after tonight. There were consequences to one's actions. You couldn't pretend to be a serious actor when you behaved very unseriously.

I closed the door, seeing the kids right behind me in the foyer. Jack was laughing uncontrollably. "Oh, Dad, that was great!" he said.

I looked at him with a sudden feeling of sadness. Only eleven years old, and already too old to believe. Innocence lasted such a short time, no matter how much we lied to prolong it.

I hoped never to have to tell Claire I drank on occasion. It would kill her.

"It's such a relief to know I can be Mormon without being perfect," Jack went on. "At church, we get yelled at for every little thing we do wrong. But here are these great men, and they're *still* great even when they're drunk."

I looked at Claire in confusion. Had the boy found my bottle in the garage? Was he talking about me? Did he mean his grandmother?

Or was he really talking about the Nephites?

"Maybe I can ask Ammon for some pot next year," he said.

"They're not Santa's helpers," Claire repeated.

"And you're not smoking pot," I said. "We've had that talk."

Jack gave me an inscrutable look. Had he found my stash as well?

He was *eleven*, for pity's sake.

"Can I turn my movie back on?" Cindy asked.

"Yeah, yeah," I replied. "You kids go watch your movie." The children returned to the living room, Jack still laughing, while I looked at Claire again in bewilderment.

"I guess we're good for another year," she whispered.

"Good grief." I wondered if I could sneak in a swig before bedtime. I always needed a little boost to get through Christmas. A swallow of mouthwash would cover it up.

But I was glad we'd put the show over on the kids for another year. I loved tradition. I squeezed Claire's hand and looked out the tiny window positioned at eye level in the door. I could just see the Three Nephites pulling away in their minivan.

I kissed Claire under the mistletoe.

Lord of the Cul de Sac

"Can't you do something, Andrew?" Marni begged. "This is Salt Lake. People are supposed to be happy here. Nice. Friendly. That guy is making life miserable for everyone."

Andrew shrugged. "It was my saying anything in the first place that caused all the trouble."

"Well, say something *else*. Make it better."

Andrew, Marni, and their four children lived on a cul de sac in Sandy, Utah. There were only five houses on their street. Four of the homes were filled with happy, life-affirming Mormons. But the house right in the middle was where Bill Niehoff lived.

The Scrooge.

The problem had started when Bill, recovering from a recent divorce, had devoted all his energy to putting up Christmas lights everywhere across his house and yard. He'd put up so many that Andrew and Marni, living right next door, couldn't sleep at night, the lights were so bright. Andrew had gone over and asked kindly, in a neighborly way, if Bill couldn't tone things down just a bit. Bill had gone ballistic.

The next evening, though, all his decorations were gone. Or rather, they'd been replaced with new decorations. Now, instead of bright lights and Santa with his reindeer and a jolly snowman, there were elves stabbing each other, Santa pissing on a stack of gifts, carolers choking one another, Mary vomiting on Jesus.

"Andrew, go talk to him," Marni begged again.

Andrew sighed and walked over to the house next door. He rang the bell. A moment later, Bill opened the door. "What do you want?" the man demanded.

"Well, it's about your decorations…" Andrew began.

"Yes?"

"Christmas is supposed to be a happy time. A time of love and understanding."

Bill leaned forward and hissed, "Merry Kiss My Ass." Then he slammed the door. Andrew walked back to his house.

"Well?" asked Marni. Andrew just shook his head.

The next day when Andrew came home from work, Marni was smiling. She gave him a peck and thrust a plate of brownies at him. "Go give these to Bill," she said. "That'll patch things up."

"Maybe we should just leave well enough alone. Christmas will be over in a couple of weeks and things will go back to normal."

"No, they won't. He'll be upset every day of the year until we resolve this." She waved the plate of brownies again. "Go on, honey."

Andrew took the plate, covered in holiday plastic wrap and topped with a bow, and headed out the door. There was a cold, stiff wind blowing, so Andrew kept his head down. He knocked on Bill's door. There was no answer. He knocked again.

"Yes?" said Bill, with a bit of a sneer. Non-Mormons could be so nasty, Andrew thought.

"My wife thought you might like some brownies." He offered the plate.

"Thanks." Bill took the brownies and closed the door.

Andrew stood there a moment, shrugged, and then walked back to his own house. At least the wind was behind him now.

"Well?" asked Marni.

"He accepted the brownies."

"And?"

"And nothing. What's for dinner?"

"Green bean casserole. It'll be ready in a few minutes. Go wash up."

Andrew and Marni and the kids were just finishing dinner when there was a loud, powerful knock on their front door. The kids jumped, and Marni looked at Andrew questioningly. Andrew went to the door and opened. Two police officers were outside.

"Can I help you?" asked Andrew.

"Your neighbor here says you gave him a plate of pot brownies."

"What!"

"The brownies tested positive. We're going to have to ask you some questions."

Andrew explained what had happened, the bad blood between them and Niehoff, and Marni's attempt to smooth things over. He explained that he was a high priest and that Marni was first counselor in the Relief Society. Three of their children were in honors classes. "Mr. Niehoff is just being…"

"A prick?" asked one of the officers.

"I was going to say 'difficult,'" Andrew said.

The officer smiled. But the two policemen seemed to accept their version of events and didn't arrest anyone. They were probably both LDS. Andrew sighed in relief as the men walked back to their car. "What are we going to do?" asked Marni as they prepared for bed later.

"We're going to leave him alone," said Andrew.

"No, we have to get through to that man somehow. We have to *do* something."

"Let's sleep on it."

When they woke up the following morning, though, and Andrew went outside to pick up the newspaper, he saw that their own modest light display had been vandalized. The wires had been cut in several places. Someone had rubbed dog feces into their wreath.

"Andrew, you've got to figure something out."

"I'm going to be late for work."

"You need to call the police."

"Maybe if we just let things drop, this will be the end of it."

"There will never be an end unless you do something."

When Andrew returned home from work that evening, Marni had a huge plateful of divinity in her hands. "Go give this to Bill," she said the moment Andrew walked through the door.

"Haven't we gone down that route already?" he asked.

"Good has *got* to prevail over evil," she replied. "We can't give up."

Andrew sighed and brought the plate of divinity over to his neighbor's house. The wind was even stronger tonight, and the temperature even lower. He hated Bill for making his life cold and miserable.

"What do you want?" Bill demanded, opening his door.

Andrew offered the plate. "We thought you might like this," he said.

Bill grabbed the plate with a wicked smile and closed the door. Andrew had a bad feeling about the exchange. He and Marni were barely finished their main course when there was another loud knock at their front door. "I told you," Andrew said.

He went to open the door and greeted the same two officers as the night before. "Yes?" he asked, trying to sound innocent, though he felt terribly guilty for some reason.

"Your neighbor here says you gave him some candy laced with LSD."

"You can't be serious," said Andrew. "Can't you guys arrest him for having all these drugs?"

"There's no evidence they're his drugs," one of the officers pointed out.

"But you know they're not ours."

The officer shrugged. "We've seen Mormons go bad before."

"This is a nightmare."

"Perhaps you'd better not give your neighbor any more gifts," said the officer.

Andrew nodded and closed the door.

"Maybe we should have the missionaries stop by," Marni suggested as they got ready for bed later. "Maybe have the ward carolers sing for him."

"I don't think that's a good idea."

"We'll, we've got to do *something*."

"We've already done something." After praying, Andrew pulled the covers up to his chin. This was like the never-ending fight between the Lamanites and Nephites, an epic battle between the positive and negative forces in the universe. It was like Frodo battling against Mordor.

It was Jesus battling Satan. And this was the season to celebrate Jesus. Jesus had to win.

In the morning, Andrew discovered that someone had turned a hose on their driveway overnight, covering the cement with a thick layer of ice. He pulled out of the driveway carefully and parked on the street after returning from work that evening. The next morning, the car itself was covered in ice.

Andrew called a cab to get to work. He thought about calling the police himself to report these incidents, but he really couldn't prove anything. The police might think he was trying to frame Niehoff, the way their neighbor was trying to implicate them.

"Andrew, we have to do something," Marni repeated when he returned from work.

"We're just going to make things worse."

"I put Bill's name on the temple prayer roll," she said.

"That's nice."

"And I made a plate of Rice Krispy treats."

"You must be kidding."

"We can't be the ones who give in first. Good has *got* to be stronger than evil."

"You already said that."

"It's still true."

Andrew sighed and carried the plate of treats next door and knocked. Bill opened with an evil gleam in his eye, chuckling as he closed the door. Andrew and Marni ate dinner in silence, waiting. Even the kids were quiet tonight. Sure enough, just as they were reaching dessert, there was a loud knock on the door.

"Yes?" Andrew asked the officers.

"We're going to have to ask you not to give any more food to your neighbor," said one of the officers. "Now he's saying you put sand in the treats. Next time, he'll claim arsenic or something, and this is really going to get out of hand. Leave him alone."

"Look what he did to my car," Andrew said. "We're just trying to be nice to the man, and he insists on being mean."

But he wondered if maybe the officers didn't have a good idea, that he should perhaps give his neighbor something with arsenic next time. He remembered the scripture, "Better that one man should perish, than a whole nation should dwindle in unbelief." Everyone on the block was starting to act nastier the past few days. Perhaps after all these episodes of crying wolf, no one would believe he and Marni had really poisoned the guy. They'd be doing a good deed.

"Stay away from him."

Andrew nodded. "I'm thinking of putting our house on the market."

"Well, wait till after Christmas. No one's going to buy if they see all his decorations."

"I heard what you said," Marni told him after he closed the door. "Are we really going to move? We're going to let that creep win?"

"Maybe it's for the best."

"Joseph Smith didn't get tired when people were awful to him. He persisted."

"He was murdered."

"We *can't* be the ones who give up," Marni insisted.

"How will it look when he takes out a restraining order against us?" He almost wanted to suggest it to Bill himself just so he'd have a reason not to let Marni keep pushing him.

Andrew suspected another attack during the night and tried to stay awake to catch his neighbor in the act. Perhaps if he had a photo proving what Bill was doing, he could press charges. But by 2:00 a.m., nothing had happened. It was like when he was a kid and trying to wait up for Santa. At a certain point, he was just too tired to keep trying.

Evil never seemed to get tired, though. Every evening, Andrew and Marni would watch a half hour of the news. And every evening, seeing all those terrible things—hostages killed in Sydney, 140 children killed in a Pakistani school, North Korea hacking into movie studios—left them feeling they were losing the battle. They'd put on a Mormon movie after dinner, trying to give their children the strength to face the world, but Andrew himself wondered how much longer he could go on.

And that was even before their neighbor became possessed by an evil spirit.

He could leave a copy of *The Power of Positive Thinking* on Bill's doorstep, but he realized the book would probably end up next to the vomit-covered Jesus, covered itself in dog poop.

But Andrew knew that Bill liked horses. He had talked about them often enough, back when he was still talking to people. Would a gift of some coffee-table book filled with beautiful horse pictures make a difference? Perhaps a replica of a Remington sculpture?

How far was Andrew willing to go? How far would Marni push him?

And why wasn't Heavenly Father helping? This was his battle, too.

In the morning, as Andrew walked groggily out to the cab, he saw that their home had been TP'd overnight, the toilet paper wrapped at intervals around the disabled Christmas lights and other vandalized decorations. All day at work, Andrew wondered what to do. His boss called him out at one point for not concentrating on his project.

When he returned home, he saw that Marni had baked a plateful of chocolate chip cookies. "No one can resist my cookies," she said, thrusting them toward Andrew. It struck Andrew suddenly that this was basically the way Heavenly

Father treated everyone on Earth, too, trying to bribe them to be good. If I give you blessings, will you follow me? There had to be a better form of motivation. Just how good could people willing to accept bribes be?

"No," he said firmly. "I'm going over to talk to him."

"Without any ammunition?"

"I'll be back in a few minutes."

Andrew walked to the house next door, his shoulders slumped. He was simply going to give in. He was going to let Bill win. It was the only solution. Maybe if Nephi hadn't behaved so arrogantly with Laman but had been gentle instead, Laman and his descendants might not have become his enemy for generations. Maybe if Joseph Smith hadn't provoked his opponents by physically attacking their printing press, he wouldn't have been shot.

Perhaps if Heavenly Father had tried being nice to Satan rather than kicking him out of heaven, things would have turned out differently. Just who was fighting whom? Who was doing the acting and who merely reacting?

Who was really the one in control?

Andrew knocked on the door. There was no answer, so he knocked again.

"Yes?" asked Bill wearily when he opened the door. He looked like a lonely, middle-aged man who just needed something bright in his life, even if it was electric.

"Bill," said Andrew. "I want to apologize. I was wrong to ask you to tone down your light display. We still have a week before Christmas. If you want, I can help you put everything back up. And I can buy you a few more lights, too, if you want. You can have the best display in all of Sandy."

Was it still a bribe if you were helping the person achieve the goals they set for themselves, rather than one you set for them?

"Won't it keep you up at night?" Bill asked with a slight tone of disgust.

"We'll put thicker blinds on our windows. What do you say?" He offered his hand.

Bill stared at Andrew for a long, long moment. Then he slowly and carefully reached out his hand as well.

Books by Johnny Townsend

Thanks for reading! If you enjoyed this book, could you please take a few minutes to write a review online? Reviews are helpful both to me as an author and to other readers, so we'd all sincerely appreciate your writing one! And if you did enjoy the book, here are some others I've written you might want to look up:

Mormon Underwear

Zombies for Jesus

A Gay Mormon Missionary in Pompeii

The Golem of Rabbi Loew

Escape from Zion

Marginal Mormons

Mormon Bullies

Bumper Sticker Theology

Going-Out-Of-Religion Sale

Gayrabian Nights

Racism by Proxy

Orgy at the STD Clinic

Life Is Better with Love

Please Evacuate

Recommended Daily Humanity

The Camper Killings

Kinky Quilts: Patchwork Designs for Gay Men

Inferno in the French Quarter: The UpStairs Lounge Fire

Latter-Gay Saints: An Anthology of Gay Mormon Fiction (co-editor)

Available from your favorite online or neighborhood bookstore.

Wondering what some of those other books are about? Read on!

Invasion of the Spirit Snatchers

During the Apocalypse, a group of Mormon survivors in Hurricane, Utah gather in the home of the Relief Society president, telling stories to pass the time as they ration their food storage and await the Second Coming. But this is no ordinary group of Mormons—or perhaps it is. They are the faithful, feminist, gay, apostate, and repentant, all working together to help each other through the darkest days any of them have yet seen.

Gayrabian Nights

Gayrabian Nights is a twist on the well-known classic, *1001 Arabian Nights*, in which Scheherazade, under the threat of death if she ceases to captivate King Shahryar's attention, enchants him through a series of mysterious, adventurous, and romantic tales.

In this variation, a male escort, invited to the hotel room of a closeted, homophobic Mormon senator, learns that the man is poised to vote on a piece of anti-gay legislation the following morning. To prevent him from sleeping, so that the exhausted senator will miss casting his vote on the Senate floor, the escort entertains him with stories of homophobia, celibacy, mixed orientation marriages, reparative therapy, coming out, first love, gay marriage, and long-term successful gay relationships. The escort crafts the stories to give the senator a crash course in gay culture and sensibilities, hoping to bring the man closer to accepting his own sexual orientation.

Inferno in the French Quarter: The UpStairs Lounge Fire

On Gay Pride Day in 1973, someone set the entrance to a French Quarter gay bar on fire. In the terrible inferno that followed, thirty-two people lost their lives, including a third of the local congregation of the Metropolitan Community Church, their pastor burning to death halfway out a second-story window as he tried to claw his way to freedom. A mother who'd gone to the bar with her two gay sons died alongside them. A man who'd helped his friend escape first was found dead near the fire escape. Two children waited outside a movie theater across town for a father and step-father who would never pick them up. During this era of rampant homophobia, several families refused to claim the bodies, and many churches refused to bury the dead. Author Johnny Townsend pored through old records and tracked down survivors of the fire as well as relatives and friends of those killed to compile this fascinating account of a forgotten moment in gay history.

A Gay Mormon Missionary in Pompeii

What is a gay Mormon missionary doing in Italy? He is trying to save his own soul as well as the souls of others. In these tales chronicling the two-year mission of Robert Anderson, we see a young man tormented by his inability to be the man the Church says he should be. In addition to his personal hell, Anderson faces a major earthquake, organized crime, a serious bus accident, and much more. He copes with horrendous mission leaders and his own suicidal tendencies. But one day, he meets another missionary who loves him, and his world changes forever.

Missionaries Make the Best Companions

What lies behind the freshly scrubbed façades of the Mormon missionaries we see about town? In these stories, an ex-Mormon tries to seduce a faithful elder by showing him increasingly suggestive movies. A sister missionary fulfills her community service requirement by babysitting for a prostitute. Two elders break their mission rules by venturing into the forbidden French Quarter. A senior missionary couple try to reactivate lapsed members while their own family falls apart back home. A young man hopes that serving a second full-time mission will lead him up the Church hierarchy. Two bored missionaries decide to make a little extra money moonlighting in a male stripper club. Two frustrated elders find an acceptable way to masturbate—by donating to a Fertility Clinic. A lonely man searches for the favorite companion he hasn't seen in thirty years.

The Golem of Rabbi Loew

Jacob and Esau Cohen are the closest of brothers. In fact, they're lovers. A doctor tries to combine canine genes with those of Jews, to improve their chances of surviving a hostile world. A Talmudic scholar dates an escort. A scientist tries to develop the "God spot" in the brains of his patients in order to create a messiah. The Golem of Prague is really Rabbi Loew's secret lover. While some of the Jews in Townsend's book are Orthodox, this collection of Jewish stories most certainly is not.

The Last Days Linger

The scriptures tell us that in the Last Days, wickedness will increase upon the Earth. When leaders of the Mormon Church see a rise in the number of gay members, they believe the end is upon them. But while "wickedness never was happiness," it begins to appear that wickedness can sometimes be divine. At least, the stories here suggest that religious proscriptions condemning homosexuality have it all wrong. While gay Mormons may be no closer to perfection than anyone else, they're no further from it, either. And sometimes, being gay provides just the right ingredient to create saints—as flawed as God himself.

Mormon Madness

Mental illness can strike the faithful as easily as anyone else. But often religious doctrine and practice exacerbate rather than alleviate these problems. From schizophrenia to obsessive-compulsive disorder, from persecution complex to sexual dysfunction, autism to dissociative identity disorder, Mormons must cope with their mental as well as their spiritual health on a daily basis.

Am I My Planet's Keeper?

Global Warming. Climate Change. Climate Crisis. Climate Emergency. Whatever label we use, we are facing one of the greatest challenges to the survival of life as we know it.

But while addressing greenhouse gases is perhaps our most urgent need, it's not our only task. We must also address toxic waste, pollution, habitat destruction, and our other contributions to the world's sixth mass extinction event.

In order to do that, we must simultaneously address the unmet human needs that keep us distracted from deeper engagement in stabilizing our climate: moderating economic inequality, guaranteeing healthcare to all, and ensuring education for everyone.

And to accomplish *that*, we must unite to combat the monied forces that use fear, prejudice, and misinformation to manipulate us.

It's a daunting task. But success is our only option.

Wake Up and Smell the Missionaries

Two Mormon missionaries in Italy discover they share the same rare ability—both can emit pheromones on demand. At first, they playfully compete in the hills of Frascati to see who can tempt "investigators" most. But soon they're targeting each other non-stop.

Can two immature young men learn to control their "superpower" to live a normal life…and develop genuine love? Even as their relationship is threatened by the attentions of another man?

They seem just on the verge of success when a massive earthquake leaves them trapped under the rubble of their apartment in Castellammare.

With night falling and temperatures dropping, can they dig themselves out in time to save themselves? And will their injuries destroy the ability that brought them together in the first place?

Orgy at the STD Clinic

Todd Tillotson is struggling to move on after his husband is killed in a hit and run attack a year earlier during a Black Lives Matter protest in Seattle.

In this novel set entirely on public transportation, we watch as Todd, isolated throughout the pandemic, battles desperation in his attempt to safely reconnect with the world.

Will he find love again, even casual friendship, or will he simply end up another crazy old man on the bus?

Things don't look good until a man whose face he can't even see sits down beside him despite the raging variants.

And asks him a question that will change his life.

Please Evacuate

A gay, partygoing New Yorker unconcerned about the future or the unsustainability of capitalism is hit by a truck and thrust into a straight man's body half a continent away. As Hunter tries to figure out what's happening, he's caught up in another disaster, a wildfire sweeping through a Colorado community, the flames overtaking him and several schoolchildren as they flee.

When he awakens, Hunter finds himself in the body of yet another man, this time in northern Italy, a former missionary about to marry a young Mormon woman. Still piecing together this new reality, and beginning to embrace his latest identity, Hunter fights for his life in a devastating flash flood along with his wife *and* his new husband.

He's an aging worker in drought-stricken Texas, a nurse at an assisted living facility in the direct path of a hurricane, an advocate for the unhoused during a freak Seattle blizzard.

We watch as Hunter is plunged into life after life, finally recognizing the futility of only looking out for #1 and understanding the part he must play in addressing the global climate crisis…if he ever gets another chance.

Recommended Daily Humanity

A checklist of human rights must include basic housing, universal healthcare, equitable funding for public schools, and tuition-free college and vocational training.

In addition to the basics, though, we need much more to fully thrive. Subsidized childcare, universal pre-K, a universal basic income, subsidized high-speed internet, net neutrality, fare-free public transit (plus *more* public transit), and medically assisted death for the terminally ill who want it.

None of this will matter, though, if we neglect to address the rapidly worsening climate crisis.

Sound expensive? It is.

But not as expensive as refusing to implement these changes. The cost of climate disasters each year has grown to staggering figures. And the cost of social and political upheaval from not meeting the needs of suffering workers, families, and individuals may surpass even that.

It's best we understand that the vast sums required to enact meaningful change are an investment which will pay off not only in some indeterminate future but in fact almost immediately. And without these adjustments to our lifestyles and values, there may very well not be a future capable of sustaining freedom and democracy…or even civilization itself.

The Camper Killings

When a homeless man is found murdered a few blocks from Morgan Beylerian's house in south Seattle, everyone seems to consider the body just so much additional trash to be cleared from the neighborhood. But Morgan liked the guy. They used to chat when Morgan brought Nick groceries once a week.

And the brutal way the man was killed reminds Morgan of their shared Mormon heritage, back when the faithful agreed to have their throats slit if they ever revealed temple secrets.

Did Nick's former wife take action when her ex-husband refused to grant a temple divorce? Did his murder have something to do with the public accusations that brought an end to his promising career?

Morgan does his best to investigate when no one else seems to care, but it isn't easy as a man living paycheck to paycheck himself, only able to pursue his investigation via public transit.

As he continues his search for the killer, Morgan's friends withdraw and his husband threatens to leave. When another homeless man is killed and Morgan is accused of the crime, things look even bleaker.

But his troubles aren't over yet.

Will Morgan find the killer before the killer finds him?

What Readers Have Said

Townsend's stories are "a gay *Portnoy's Complaint* of Mormonism. Salacious, sweet, sad, insightful, insulting, religiously ethnic, quirky-faithful, and funny."

D. Michael Quinn, author of *The Mormon Hierarchy: Origins of Power*

"Told from a believably conversational first-person perspective, [*A Gay Mormon Missionary in Pompeii*'s] novelistic focus on Anderson's journey to thoughtful self-acceptance allows for greater character development than often seen in short stories, which makes this well-paced work rich and satisfying, and one of Townsend's strongest. An extremely important contribution to the field of Mormon fiction." Named to Kirkus Reviews' Best of 2011.

Kirkus Reviews

"The thirteen stories in *Mormon Underwear* capture this struggle [between Mormonism and homosexuality] with humor, sadness, insight, and sometimes shocking details….*Mormon Underwear* provides compelling stories, literally from the inside-out."

Niki D'Andrea, *Phoenix New Times*

"Townsend's lively writing style and engaging characters [in *Zombies for Jesus*] make for stories which force us to wake up, smell the (prohibited) coffee, and review our attitudes with regard to reading dogma so doggedly. These are tales which revel in the individual tics and quirks which make us human, Mormon or not, gay or not..."

A.J. Kirby, *The Short Review*

"The Rift," from *A Gay Mormon Missionary in Pompeii*, is a "fascinating tale of an untenable situation...a *tour de force*."

David Lenson, editor, *The Massachusetts Review*

"Pronouncing the Apostrophe," from *The Golem of Rabbi Loew*, is "quiet and revealing, an intriguing tale..."

Sima Rabinowitz, Literary Magazine Review, *NewPages.com*

The Circumcision of God is "a collection of short stories that consider the imperfect, silenced majority of Mormons, who may in fact be [the Church's] best hope....[The book leaves] readers regretting the church's willingness to marginalize those who best exemplify its ideals: those who love fiercely despite all obstacles, who brave challenges at great personal risk and who always choose the hard, higher road."

Kirkus Reviews

In *Mormon Fairy Tales*, Johnny Townsend displays "both a wicked sense of irony and a deep well of compassion."

Kel Munger, *Sacramento News and Review*

Zombies for Jesus is "eerie, erotic, and magical."

Publishers Weekly

"While [Townsend's] many touching vignettes draw deeply from Mormon mythology, history, spirituality and culture, [*Mormon Fairy Tales*] is neither a gaudy act of proselytism nor angry protest literature from an ex-believer. Like all good fiction, his stories are simply about the joys, the hopes and the sorrows of people."

Kirkus Reviews

"In *Inferno in the French Quarter* author Johnny Townsend restores this tragic event [the UpStairs Lounge fire] to its proper place in LGBT history and reminds us that the victims of the blaze were not just 'statistics,' but real people with real lives, families, and friends."

Jesse Monteagudo, *The Bilerico Project*

In *Inferno in the French Quarter*, "Townsend's heart-rending descriptions of the victims…seem to [make them] come alive once more."

Kit Van Cleave, *OutSmart Magazine*

Marginal Mormons is "an irreverent, honest look at life outside the mainstream Mormon Church….Throughout his musings on sin and forgiveness, Townsend beautifully demonstrates his characters' internal, perhaps irreconcilable struggles….Rather than anger and disdain, he offers an honest portrayal of people searching for meaning and community in their lives, regardless of their life choices or secrets." Named to Kirkus Reviews' Best of 2012.

Kirkus Reviews

The stories in *The Mormon Victorian Society* "register the new openness and confidence of gay life in the age of same-sex marriage….What hasn't changed is Townsend's wry, conversational prose, his subtle evocations of character and social dynamics, and his deadpan humor. His warm empathy still glows in this intimate yet clear-eyed engagement with Mormon theology and folkways. Funny, shrewd and finely wrought dissections of the awkward contradictions—and surprising harmonies—between conscience and desire." Named to Kirkus Reviews' Best of 2013.

Kirkus Reviews

"This collection of short stories [*The Mormon Victorian Society*] featuring gay Mormon characters slammed [me] in the face from the first page, wrestled my heart and mind to the floor, and left me panting and wanting more by the end. Johnny Townsend has created so many memorable characters in such few pages. I went weeks thinking about this book. It truly touched me."

Tom Webb, *A Bear on Books*

Dragons of the Book of Mormon is an "entertaining collection….Townsend's prose is sharp, clear, and easy to read, and his characters are well rendered…"

Publishers Weekly

"The pre-eminent documenter of alternative Mormon lifestyles…Townsend has a deep understanding of his characters, and his limpid prose, dry humor and well-grounded (occasionally magical) realism make their spiritual conundrums both compelling and entertaining. [*Dragons of the Book of Mormon* is] [a]nother of Townsend's critical but affectionate and absorbing tours of Mormon discontent." Named to Kirkus Reviews' Best of 2014.

Kirkus Reviews

In *Gayrabian Nights*, "Townsend's prose is always limpid and evocative, and…he finds real drama and emotional depth in the most ordinary of lives."

Kirkus Reviews

Gayrabian Nights "was easily the most original book I've read all year. Funny, touching, topical, and thoroughly enjoyable."

Rainbow Awards

Lying for the Lord is "one of the most gripping books that I've picked up for quite a while. I love the author's writing style, alternately cynical, humorous, biting, scathing, poignant, and touching…. This is the third book of his that I've read, and all are equally engaging. These are stories that need to be told, and the author does it in just the right way."

Heidi Alsop, *Ex-Mormon Foundation Board Member*

In *Lying for the Lord*, Townsend "gets under the skin of his characters to reveal their complexity and conflicts….shrewd, evocative [and] wryly humorous."

Kirkus Reviews

In *Missionaries Make the Best Companions*, "the author treats the clash between religious dogma and liberal humanism with vivid realism, sly humor, and subtle feeling as his characters try to figure out their true missions in life. Another of Townsend's rich dissections of Mormon failures and uncertainties…" Named to Kirkus Reviews' Best of 2015.

Kirkus Reviews

In *Invasion of the Spirit Snatchers*, "Townsend, a confident and practiced storyteller, skewers the hypocrisies and eccentricities of his characters with precision and affection. The outlandish framing narrative is the most consistent source of shock and humor, but the stories do much to ground the reader in the world—or former world—of the characters….A funny, charming tale about a group of Mormons facing the end of the world."

Kirkus Reviews

"Townsend's collection [*The Washing of Brains*] once again displays his limpid, naturalistic prose, skillful narrative chops, and his subtle insights into psychology…Well-crafted dispatches on the clash between religion and self-fulfillment…"

Kirkus Reviews

"While the author is generally at his best when working as a satirist, there are some fine, understated touches in these tales [*The Last Days Linger*] that will likely affect readers in subtle ways….readers should come away impressed by the deep empathy he shows for all his characters—even the homophobic ones."

Kirkus Reviews

"Written in a conversational style that often uses stories and personal anecdotes to reveal larger truths, this immensely approachable book [*Racism by Proxy*] skillfully serves its intended audience of White readers grappling with complex questions regarding race, history, and identity. The author's frequent references to the Church of Jesus Christ of Latter-day Saints may be too niche for readers unfamiliar with its idiosyncrasies, but Townsend generally strikes a perfect balance of humor, introspection, and reasoned arguments that will engage even skeptical readers."

Kirkus Reviews

Orgy at the STD Clinic portrays "an all-too real scenario that Townsend skewers to wincingly accurate proportions…[with] instant classic moments courtesy of his punchy, sassy, sexy lead character…"

Jim Piechota, *Bay Area Reporter*

Orgy at the STD Clinic is "…a triumph of humane sensibility. A richly textured saga that brilliantly captures the fraying social fabric of contemporary life." Named to Kirkus Reviews' Best Indie Books of 2022.

Kirkus Reviews

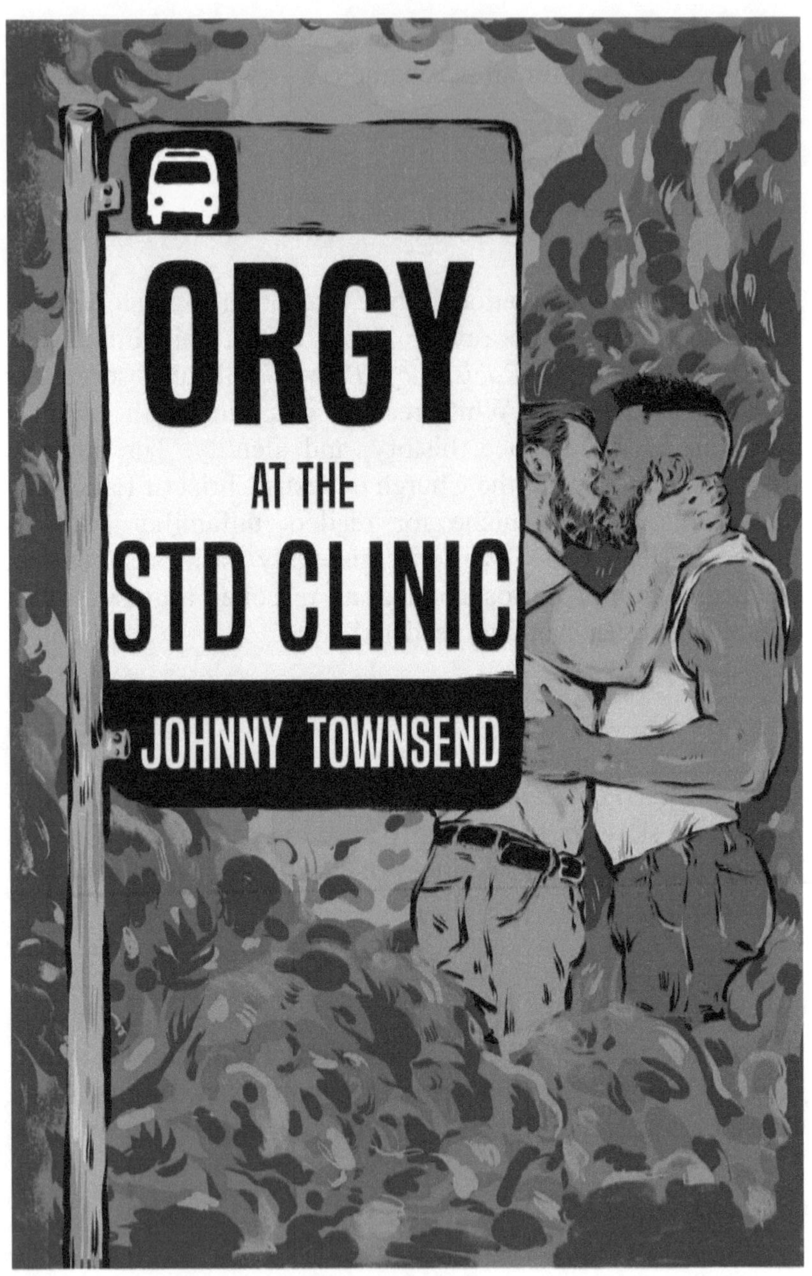

ORGY
AT THE
STD CLINIC
JOHNNY TOWNSEND

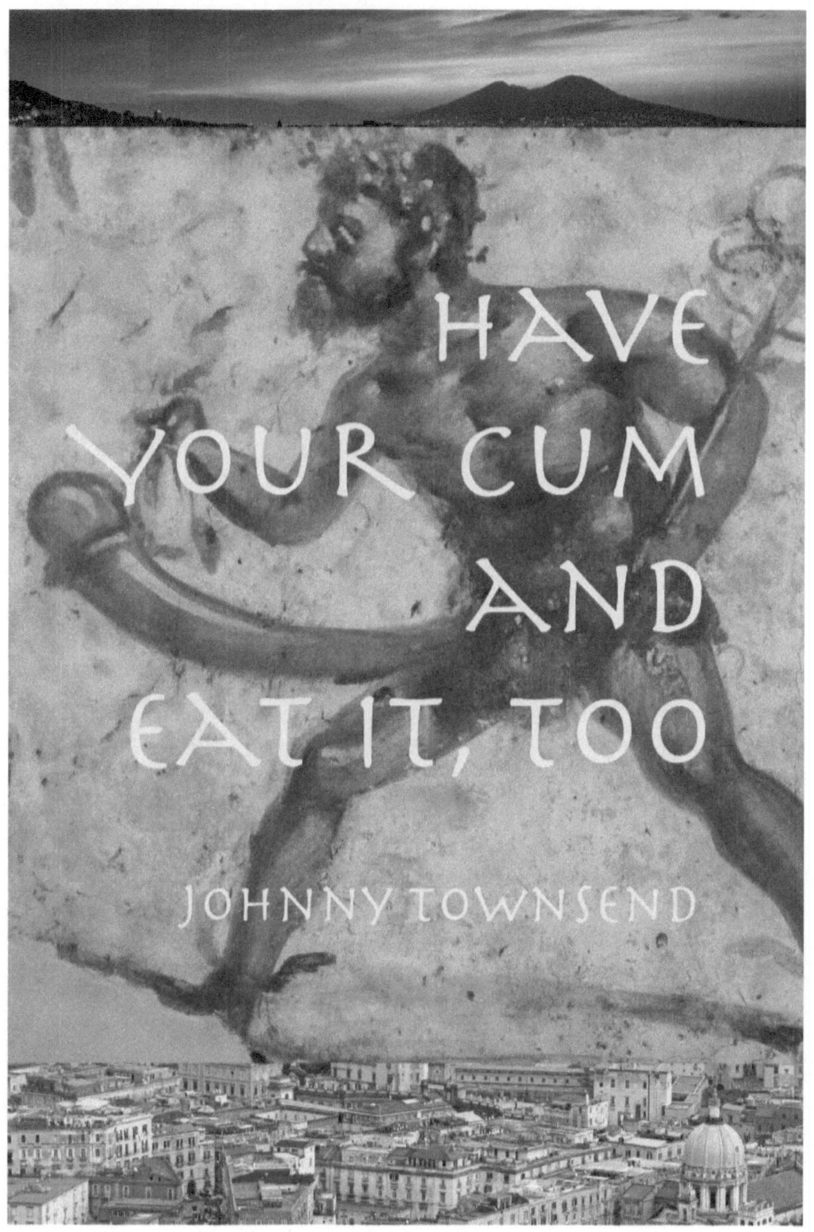
HAVE
YOUR CUM
AND
EAT IT, TOO
JOHNNY TOWNSEND

Going-Out-Of-
Religion Sale
JOHNNY TOWNSEND